# NAKED AMBITION

Robert Gott was born in the Queensland town of Maryborough and lives in Melbourne. He has published many books for children, written two series of historical crime novels, and is also the creator of the newspaper cartoon *The Adventures of Naked Man*.

# Robert
# GOTT

# Naked
# AMBITION

SCRIBE
*Melbourne • London*

Scribe Publications
18–20 Edward St, Brunswick, Victoria 3056, Australia
2 John St, Clerkenwell, London, WC1N 2ES, United Kingdom
3754 Pleasant Ave, Suite 100, Minneapolis, Minnesota 55409,
USA

First published by Scribe 2023

Typeset in Adobe Caslon Pro by the publishers.

Printed and bound in the UK by CPI Group (UK) Ltd, Croydon
CR0 4YY

Scribe is committed to the sustainable use of natural resources
and the use of paper products made responsibly from those
resources.

978 1 957363 61 5 (US edition)
978 1 922585 96 7 (Australian edition)
978 1 761385 14 8 (ebook)

scribepublications.com
scribepublications.com.au
scribepublications.co.uk

*For my late parents, Maurene and Kevin. Always.*

# Part
# ONE

The package that emerged from the back of the delivery van was much larger and heavier than Gregory Buchanan was expecting. Well, he knew it was going to be big — this wasn't the first time he'd seen it — but he didn't remember it being *this* big. It was awkward manoeuvring it into the house, with the help of the van driver. Later, of course, its size would prove to be the least awkward thing about it. He thanked the delivery chap and leaned the great object against the wall of the dining room. It was wrapped in protective layers of opaque plastic, which Gregory removed, strip by strip, until the object was revealed. He stepped back from it and worried that his initial response was trepidation. This was quickly suppressed in favour of celebration. Yes, he thought, it's beautiful, and to reassure himself that this was true, he said it out loud.

'It's beautiful.'

When Phoebe saw it, she'd be bowled over. Gregory was confident that she wouldn't just like it; she'd admire it.

When Phoebe first met Gregory, it wasn't love at first sight. An accumulation of sightings led finally to marriage. Phoebe couldn't say for certain that this slow accretion had also led to love. She wasn't sure what love was, or what it might feel like. She had always assumed that one of its hallmarks was constancy, and there was nothing constant about her feelings for Gregory. He was attractive. She liked touching him, and liked being touched by him. There were aspects of Gregory, however, that even after eight years of marriage she found unappealing.

One of Gregory's idiosyncrasies — the one that really got up her nose — was his belief that Phoebe's mother liked him, and that she was a perfectly reasonable woman, if a bit unmoveable on questions of religion. Phoebe's mother, Joyce, was not a reasonable person and she loathed Gregory. His inability to see this made Phoebe wonder sometimes if he wasn't a little bit stupid. It wasn't stupidity, though. She'd come to realise over time what it was. It was vanity. Gregory was constitutionally incapable of grasping the idea that anyone could dislike him. His failure to notice his mother-in-law's disdain was astonishing to Phoebe. She'd grown up in its chilly atmosphere. She'd known from an early age that Joyce's love of Jesus was so exhausting that only unpalatable scraps of love were available for her, and, she presumed, her father. He'd died when she was just ten years old, and she had no real sense of him. When she thought about him, she wondered if he'd accepted the cancer that killed him as a medical ticket-of-leave. He went swiftly and didn't put up a fight.

Her mother's ministry, as Joyce liked to call it, swept around and over Phoebe, but it was a miasma, not a flood, and it failed to sweep her away. She grew up, therefore, with daily reminders that she was not only a disappointment, but proof that the devil was abroad in the world. Joyce came to accept Phoebe's early-onset atheism as a cross that tested her and secured her own faith. When faced with Phoebe's defiance, she learned to meet it with a dead bat. When truly exasperated, she would say, 'You have been sent to test my endurance, but if He can lead me to it, He can lead me through it.' And so Phoebe's difficult teenage years weren't as explosive as they might otherwise have been. Mother and daughter assumed a sort of détente. They were mostly civil to each other. Phoebe moved out of home as soon as she turned eighteen, and Joyce even helped her along with a large gift of money.

'Your father and I put this aside for your eighteenth birthday.'

Phoebe had been unexpectedly touched by this, and she'd hugged her mother. Joyce had been so surprised by this sudden expression of affection that she'd become rigid. Phoebe later recalled that it was like wrapping her arms round a telephone pole, and it quickly became the subject of an anecdote she called the 'hugging incident'.

In the course of their courtship, Phoebe and Gregory had decided that, on balance, they were sufficiently compatible to risk marriage. The decision to marry puzzled many of their friends, but what these friends didn't know was that Gregory and Phoebe shared a secret conservative bent. It wasn't conservative enough to frighten the horses, but it was definitely there. They lived together for two years before they got married, so it wasn't *that* kind of conservatism. Indeed, it was the decision to live together in a de facto relationship that permanently alienated Joyce from Gregory. Two years of obliging her daughter to live as the Whore of Babylon would require a lifetime of hard penance, and Gregory showed no inclination towards contrition. He was among the damned. Well Phoebe was among the damned too, of course, but Joyce held onto an unexpressed hope that her own fierce faith would go some way towards softening the Lord's treatment of Phoebe on Judgement Day.

Phoebe had a talent for PR and she exercised this talent in an unofficial capacity by overseeing Gregory's move from an Arts degree into the more practical, if drab, world of local politics and then into state politics, where Gregory's election took even him by surprise. She hadn't exactly supervised his campaign, but she'd double-checked all of his speeches and managed his wardrobe and haircut. He'd wanted to grow a moustache for Movember, and Phoebe reminded him that he'd grown a moustache when they'd first got married and that they'd agreed that he looked like a sex offender and that they'd never revisit the experiment or speak of it again. This became known as the 'moustache incident'.

Gregory worked hard in his first two years in parliament, although he was conscious of the fact that he was too young to be taken seriously. His party was also in opposition, so his profile was low. Nevertheless, with Phoebe at his side, they worked for his electorate assiduously, turning up at every frightful community event to which they were invited. They were an attractive couple, and Phoebe taught Gregory how to lean towards the person who was speaking to him, hold his or her eyes, and create an effective illusion of engaged listening.

'If you simply repeat something they say, they think they've won you over.'

Gregory got so used to doing this that he occasionally fell into doing it at home. Whenever this happened, Phoebe would leave off what she'd been saying, walk into the kitchen and return with a jug of water, which she would empty into Gregory's lap. He was a slow learner, so the lesson didn't take until the third dousing, even though Phoebe had said, 'Every time you do that to me, the water will get hotter.'

An early election was called during Gregory's third

year in parliament, the fixed term of four years having been altered with bipartisan support. Both major parties preferred to re-arm themselves with the weapon of an expedient and sudden election. And not only was Gregory returned to office, though the margin was tight, but he found himself in government, his party having snatched the prize after preferences. He was now seen as someone to watch. He won his seat in the subsequent election too, although with an even tighter margin. Once the business of government was underway, people tended to forget about margins, at least until they were reminded of it at the next election.

So, in the eighth year of their marriage, and in another election year, Gregory had been promoted to the position of minister for transport, which was something of a poisoned chalice. People blamed you for traffic. Still, it was generally agreed that he was doing a good job. And despite the demands of the job, Phoebe and Gregory's partnership was solid.

The first real test of their marriage arose out of the 'portrait incident'.

On the morning the object arrived, they stood in front of where Gregory had hung it on the dining-room wall. He had in mind that this would be its temporary home. Ultimately, it would hang in the living room. Just at the moment the hook in the dining room was the only one able to accommodate its size and weight. Phoebe stared up at it and for far too long failed to say anything.

Eventually, she said, 'You're a politician, a public figure. What on earth were you thinking?'

Gregory had been expecting enthusiasm, and he was, frankly, a little miffed.

'I was thinking that I'd like an honest portrait of myself. What I didn't want was a flattering, obsequious, bland job.'

'Well full marks for honesty, darling, only I don't think you mentioned that you were commissioning a nude portrait.'

'I wanted that to be a surprise.'

'We've been married for eight years. The element of surprise is somewhat muted.'

Gregory stood back from the painting and ran his eyes over it, from top to bottom. Phoebe stepped back to stand beside him.

She said, 'It's much larger than I expected. The scale I mean. Obviously.'

'Portraits have a way of making the familiar unfamiliar, don't you think? She's a great admirer of Sir Joshua Reynolds, and Bronzino. It's sort of an homage to Bronzino's *Portrait of a Young Man*. Sophie talked a lot about Bronzino during our sessions.'

Phoebe turned to Gregory and found him lost in admiration of the painting. She stepped in front of him and stared into his face. He was bewildered by this sudden severing of his connection with the portrait.

'I'm sorry,' she said. 'What did you just say?'

'Bronzino. Sophie admires Bronzino.'

'I see. And which of those two names do you think I might be interested in knowing about?'

'Have you heard of Bronzino?'

Phoebe remained calm. She turned, walked to the painting, leaned down to examine the bottom, left corner, and read, 'Sophie White.' She smiled at Gregory. 'Sophie White. I've heard the name, but not from you. You didn't actually mention that you were being painted by a woman.'

'I'm sure I must have mentioned it.'

'No, darling, you didn't. So when you went off to her studio, that's how each sitting went, with you, stark naked and standing like that.'

Gregory skirted the issue.

'It mimics the Bronzino pose. Sophie White is an artist, Phoebe. That's like being a doctor. It's what she does, all day, every day. She doesn't see bodies the way civilians do.'

'Civilians?'

'Sophie sees non-artists as civilians. She sees a lot of other artists as civilians too. She has high standards.'

'Oh, well, that's all right then.'

Gregory, perhaps as proof that his astuteness was unpredictable — or more correctly, unreliable in its app-lication — could not understand his wife's tepid response.

'You haven't actually said what you think about it,' he said.

With bracing bluntness, Phoebe said, 'I think it's ghastly and the additional information you've reluctantly supplied doesn't help my appreciation.'

Gregory was taken aback.

'Ghastly? Ghastly? Are we looking at the same painting? Pretend it's not me. Pretend it's a stranger. Try to see it objectively.'

'It's a little difficult to pretend it's not you. It's not exactly abstract expressionism, is it? It's practically photographic.'

'But look at the creamy application of the paint, the way she manages the lights and darks.'

Phoebe knew that Gregory was teetering on the edge of saying 'chiaroscuro' in an affected Italian accent, and she thought she'd run screaming from the room if he did this, so she tried to change tack.

'Seriously, Gregory, what were you thinking? What are our friends going to say about it? And my mother. Well, we know what she'll say. The one advantage of having a religious maniac for a mother is that you always know exactly what she's going to say, and that it will be offensive and stupid.'

'Joyce might surprise you.'

There it was — that annoying, pointless, exasperating defence of her mother.

'Mum hasn't surprised me since … No, she's never surprised me.'

Gregory walked towards the painting, then away

from it, then towards it again.

'It doesn't matter whether people approve or disapprove. It's a work of art. It's not the job of art to court approval.'

'Have you noticed that the focal point of the picture is your penis? It's where the eye falls first. Also, once you get to your face, you have a smug look on it.'

'I don't see that at all. I look confident, yes. It's a sort of swagger portrait. I'm supposed to look self-assured.'

'Well you look smug instead, and that's not quite the same thing.'

This wasn't going the way Gregory had hoped it would go. He'd thought that Phoebe would be a little shocked and then applaud his daring.

'You really hate it, don't you?'

Phoebe reached out and took Gregory's hand. He accepted the gesture, but his squeeze lacked conviction.

'As a general rule,' Phoebe said, 'I think it's a mistake to have your face and your genitals in the same portrait, because like it or not, people will be more interested in your penis than your face. They can see your face anytime.'

'And my penis only on special occasions?'

'Or perhaps preferably not at all, unless you present it to them on a platter, like that.'

Gregory extracted his hand.

'I'm astonished, Phoebe, that you're being so prudish.'

'I'm not being prudish. I've been in PR for a long time, and something like this has to be managed, not sprung on people. Lots of people come to this house, and someone is bound to take a photo and pass it around on social media, and before you know it, before you can *control* it, it's on the front page of a Murdoch toilet roll.'

Gregory was about to say something but thought better of it. He walked towards the kitchen and returned with a glass of water. He'd drunk half of it before he realised that Phoebe was watching him.

'I'm sorry, did you want some water?'

'Apparently not.'

Phoebe was suddenly cross with herself. She didn't want a glass of water, so making it a casus belli was pointless. She knew it was transferred annoyance over the painting. She crossed her arms.

'Tell me about Sophie White.'

'She's an important, established artist.'

'Aged?'

'I don't know. Does it matter?'

'Not if she's ninety.'

It was a habit of Gregory's to miss the red flags Phoebe sometimes waved at him, and he was unwary.

'She's in her thirties, I think. Early thirties.'

'And how did the conversation that ended with "Take your clothes off" begin?'

Gregory finally caught a glimpse of the flag.

'*I* suggested I wanted something out of the ordinary,

something that spoke about me as a man, not just another politician.'

'So the nude thing was your idea?'

'I'm not sure whether she suggested it or I did. Surely that's not important. The point is, she's made the cut for the Archibald twice.'

He finished the glass of water before adding, 'She wants to enter this in the Archibald.'

Phoebe's eyebrows shot up and she placed the palm of her hand on Gregory's chest.

'Of course, you told her that that's out of the question. You're the minister for transport. No one who doesn't have to wants to see the minister for transport naked.'

Gregory, with the air of someone who believed he was delivering a trump card, said, 'Glenda Jackson was the minister for London transport in the Blair government. She took her clothes off in *The Music Lovers*. In fact, she rolls around naked on the floor of a train, which was prescient.'

Phoebe tried to make sense of this. She wasn't entirely successful.

'Glenda Jackson in a turgid Ken Russell film from 1970 is not a precedent for a portrait of an Australian member of parliament in the nude, and especially not in an election year. Australians don't like their politicians with their clothes *on*. Taking them off isn't going to win you any votes.'

Gregory thought about that for a moment. There was a good deal of truth in what Phoebe said, but with his portrait now before him, imposing in its scale, and emphatic in its nakedness, he felt that he had to hold the line, although he did experience a small stab that he might be accused of exhibitionism, and this caught him off guard.

'I'm not ashamed of my body. Are you saying I should be ashamed of my body?'

The weakness of this argument was so self-evident that Phoebe didn't have the heart to laugh. Gregory's face had assumed a pleading look that was simultaneously repugnant and endearing.

'I think you know that you're missing the point. This isn't about your body. It's a fine body. Look at it. A thing of beauty and a wonder to behold.'

'Thank you.'

'However,' Phoebe said with careful emphasis, 'in the middle of all that beauty, at eye level in fact, there is what is inescapably a penis.' She leaned into the picture. 'And she's even painted that small freckle on your scrotum. She must have got close to notice that.'

Gregory peered at his painted scrotum.

'I didn't know that was there.'

'Well now everyone knows.'

Neither Phoebe nor Gregory heard the front door open and close, and they were so focused on the painting that they were deaf to the opening of the living-room door also. As Gregory was considering what to say about this freckle and the clearly forensic examination Sophie White had made of his body, his mother, Margaret, put her bag down on the living-room sofa. From where Gregory and Phoebe were standing in the dining room, Margaret couldn't be seen.

Margaret Buchanan was approaching seventy, reluctantly — a reluctance eased by what she considered remedial doses of gin and tonic. She'd never appeared falling-down drunk at a family event, although Gregory and Phoebe had often confiscated her car keys and insisted that she stay the night. On such occasions she would confect outrage and insist that the amount of gin she had drunk was practically homeopathic in its strength and effect. The truth was, she quite liked staying the night. She was fond of Phoebe, and the tendency she had towards nosiness meant that she was fascinated by Phoebe's upbringing, and by Phoebe's mother, Joyce. She'd met Joyce a few times, none of them without incident. Margaret was not a religious woman. Her prophets were Christopher Hitchens and Richard Dawkins, and Joyce seemed as unspeakable and dangerous and weird as one of Macbeth's witches. It was Margaret's ambition to one day take her down with blistering, well-researched, and brilliant argument.

Now the question of Gregory's freckle had created a moment of silence in the dining room. This was broken when Phoebe said, 'The penis is the problem. It's the problem generally, of course, but in this instance your penis is specifically the problem.'

Margaret stood stock-still in the living room.

'What's wrong with my penis?'

'Oh for God's sake. This isn't about whether your penis is a good penis or a bad penis.'

'Are you saying it's not an attractive penis?'

'There's no such thing as an attractive penis.'

Margaret thought about leaving but opted instead to announce her arrival by saying loudly, 'Can you both please stop saying the word "penis"? It's hideous.'

She didn't move towards the dining room, thinking that she ought to give Gregory time to put his penis away, because the fact that it was under discussion suggested that it was on view. Why he should have it out in the dining room was puzzling. Perhaps they'd been making love on the table. She hoped not. The thought of it would spoil the next Sunday roast. Phoebe came into the living room. She was unflustered and smiled at Margaret, who was instantly reassured that she hadn't caught them in flagrante delicto.

'You should have let us know that you were here, Margaret.'

'Yes, I am so sorry. I really ought to knock.'

Gregory came into the room, and Margaret couldn't stop herself from checking his trousers for evidence of hurried tucking. He noticed this and put his hands on his hips defiantly. Margaret had the grace to be slightly embarrassed, and covered it by being forthright.

'What is wrong with Gregory's private parts? They used to be perfectly normal. If there's something odd about them now, it's got nothing to do with my parenting. He left home in full working order.'

Phoebe kissed her mother-in-law on the cheek and marvelled at the difference between this woman and her own mother.

'You haven't developed an unsightly growth, have you? I was a nurse, remember. I've seen things that would curl your hair.'

Gregory laughed and kissed his mother hello.

'There's nothing wrong with my private parts. Yes, I know. How disappointing. Phoebe and I were discussing aesthetics, not pathology. You can see what the fuss is about on the wall in the dining room.'

Phoebe put her arm around Margaret's shoulder and steered her towards a viewing.

'Gregory has had his portrait painted, and he wants to hang it in the Archibald.'

Margaret was genuinely pleased, and her immediate thought was that of course it must win. The son of one of her closest friends had been the subject of an Archibald portrait, and that picture had won. Margaret had been effusive at the time, but her real feeling was that neither the sitter nor his portrait was anything to write home about. It was a likeness of sorts, but that really didn't make it attractive or worthy.

'Oh, how lovely,' she said. 'When you become prime minister, you'll have to give it to the nation.'

'The words "grateful nation" don't spring to mind, Margaret.'

'It's not one of those horrid abstract things that look like someone suffering a Tourette's episode was involved in it, is it? I hope it at least looks like ...' Margaret reached the portrait. 'Oh, my goodness.'

'You have to admit it's a good likeness, Mum.'

'I'm sorry, I haven't got to the face yet. The eye gets rather snagged, doesn't it?'

Margaret struggled to maintain the veneer of modernity and acceptance of which she was so proud, and in which she sort of believed. Gregory came and stood beside her. He wasn't indifferent to the fact that his mother was staring at his naked body, but suppressed his discomfort. He certainly wasn't going to acknowledge it.

'Try not to look at it in sections. Take it all in. The colours. The tonal shifts. The chiaroscuro.'

Phoebe winced at the sound of that word, or rather at Gregory's ostentatiously Italian pronunciation of it.

'I'll get us some drinks. Is it too early for a gin and tonic for you, Margaret?'

'I almost feel like it's too late for a gin and tonic. I think we've done this in the wrong order, but yes, please. A gin and tonic would be helpful at this point.'

Phoebe went into the kitchen. Margaret and

Gregory stood in silent contemplation of the painting.

'You disapprove, don't you?'

'Well it's …'

'It's me, Mum. That's all. It's me. Is that so very shocking?'

'You didn't think about a little manscaping before you … ?'

'Oh for God's sake, Mum. Is that seriously all you've got to say? This was painted by Sophie White. It's a coup to be painted by her, and it cost a bomb, but I have no doubt that it's already worth more than I paid for it. She is a major, major artist.'

Margaret returned to the living room and sat down on the sofa. Gregory leaned in the dining-room doorway.

'I suppose if it stays within the confines of this house until after your death, perhaps a hundred years after your death, it will do no harm, and if Phoebe is happy to live with it, there's nothing more to be said.'

Reluctant to *not* say any more, she added, 'If your father had brought a picture of himself like that home, we may at some point have had sex again, but possibly not with each other.'

Margaret hadn't had many arguments with her children while they were growing up. Gregory had argued with his father; the disagreements had never been violent, and the heat had gone out of them quickly. Often, hours after a row, Barry would turn to his wife in bed and wonder out loud if Gregory's combination of stubbornness and stupidity was genetically determined and permanent.

'It's amazing, isn't it,' Margaret would say, 'that reason and brilliance should produce such a mutation?'

'It's a recessive gene. He's a throwback to your father and my mother.'

Margaret was wondering how Barry would deal with this situation when Gregory said, with just a hint of leftover petulance from his younger self, 'You're shocked. You're actually shocked. Why? There I am, presented simply and honestly as a human being. Well how very, very shocking. Sophie White is right. Someone has to challenge society's prudery and hypocrisy. One of the reasons I got into politics in the first place was to challenge hypocrisy and cant.'

Margaret, who'd yet to see any evidence of this challenge in her son's public life, chose not to query him on this.

'That's all very well, but if that picture is paraded in the Archibald Prize, you'll never be prime minister, and you probably won't be re-elected, and this government can't afford to lose a single seat. There is nothing noble in what you're doing.'

Despite the fact that his mother had spoken relatively calmly, Gregory said, 'That's a hysterical response.'

'If ever I become hysterical, darling, you will know

about it, because it usually involves a nosebleed, and it's usually not my nose doing the bleeding. I think it's safe to say that Australians are fairly indifferent to their prime ministers' looks — how else can you explain the parade of gargoyles that have held that office — but they are unlikely to be indifferent to a display of prime-ministerial pudenda. The scrotum is not a vote winner.'

That statement hung in the air for a moment, like a speech balloon in a cartoon. Gregory tried to reassure himself that it sounded truer than it actually was.

Phoebe returned during this break in hostilities with the drinks — three gin and tonics. She presented the tray to Margaret and directed her choice.

'I've made yours a bit stronger. I know you always say that the gin is the tonic. It's the one on the left.'

Margaret took the drink and sipped it immediately.

'I've been giving Gregory some practical advice,' she said. 'A little realpolitik.'

Gregory sat in the armchair opposite his mother. Phoebe stayed standing. She looked at Gregory and tried to gauge how far down the path of stubbornness he'd wandered. She could always tell by the set of his mouth. A couple of years back, after the moustache incident, he'd embarked upon the growth of what he'd hoped would be a big beard. They'd had words. Growing a beard was not a skill, she'd said, and a beard hid the mouth.

'How can I tell if you're smirking if I can't see your mouth?'

In the end, the beard lost, mainly because Gregory realised that it wasn't being admired in his electorate. He'd trimmed it, and neatened it, but it was too late. The trimmed beard triggered people into remembering the big beard, so he'd returned to the tyranny of the daily, sometimes twice-daily shave. This brought an end to the beard incident.

'So,' he said after taking a gulp of his gin and tonic, 'we might have to agree to disagree on this one. I'm happy with the painting, more than happy. I'm thrilled with it. And I would make the point that it's my body and that I'm perfectly comfortable with it, and that should be all that matters. Surely.'

'It's taking transparency in government too far,' Margaret said.

'Look, I'll be perfectly frank with you. The more you and Phoebe disapprove, the more committed I am to showing the picture.'

Phoebe brought her glass to her mouth sharply in order to stop up the rush of words she wanted to hurl at Gregory. He continued.

'Sophie White predicted that this would happen.'

'That hardly makes her clairvoyant,' Margaret said.

'She said that even people close to me would be so confronted and outraged that they'd try to make *me* feel embarrassed, when in fact it's *they* who are embarrassed and not nearly as liberal minded as they like to think they are.'

He gestured towards the dining room.

'This is an important painting and showing it might also be an important moment in the maturation of this country. For a start, only a handful of women have ever won the Archibald, something like eight over one hundred years, which is ludicrous. When Nora Heysen won it in 1938, Max Meldrum said that women simply couldn't be expected to paint as well as men. And there have been only a tiny number of nude portraits that have ever been selected as finalists, and a nude portrait has never won. We haven't really come very far from 1938, have we? It would be cowardly, disrespectful, and hypocritical not to stand by the painting's obvious merits. I believe, I *firmly* believe, that the electorate, *my* electorate, will see that a politician with courage is a politician who'll tell them the truth. This portrait puts me beyond the suspicion of spin. This emperor *knows* he has no clothes. I want people to trust me, and I am unashamedly naked before them.'

Gregory felt pleased by the rhetorical flourish of that final statement.

Phoebe said, 'They didn't like your beard. They're not going to like your pubes.'

'However impressive they are,' Margaret said.

'If you really want a frank assessment of your portrait,' Phoebe said, 'I'll give you one. No beating about the bush.'

'However impressive it is.'

'This is non-judgemental, public-relations advice. This is what I do for a living, Gregory. I give advice to people who need someone else to give them that advice because they have no idea what's best for them, and I am trying, I am *really* trying not to patronise you, but in the dining room there is a full-length, larger-than-life portrait of the minister for transport, naked. *And* the minister in question thinks this might be a good advertisement for him and for the teetering government he represents. In an election year. Under these circumstances, it's very difficult not to be patronising, because the minister's position on this beggars belief. The problem with your portrait, apart from the screamingly obvious one, is that it's hideous.'

Gregory's mouth opened involuntarily. Margaret wasn't tempted to interrupt, which was something of a first. Phoebe in full flight was a little intimidating.

'I'm not saying it's not a good likeness, in the sense that it's clearly and unambiguously you, but somehow Sophie White has put something into your face that isn't there in real life. You look smug, self-important, and ugly, and you're none of those things. I think you've been taken in by Sophie White, and I think she hates you and everything you stand for. People will see that and wonder why on earth you submitted to it.'

There was silence. Gregory said, quietly, 'That's absurd.'

Margaret, who'd finished her gin and tonic, was

beginning to feel uncomfortable. She'd never seen Phoebe and Gregory argue before. She'd seen them bicker, but this felt as if it could spiral out of control.

With contrived calm, Gregory said, 'I think you're peeved that I posed for her. I think you're jealous.'

With equally contrived calm, Phoebe said, 'How very interesting that you would assume I might be jealous. Is there something I need to be jealous of?'

Margaret felt that this was worse than shouting and that Phoebe and Gregory seemed to have forgotten that she was there, privy to the awful intimacy of this exchange.

'Please, Phoebe, Gregory, let's not get sidetracked by the aesthetic strengths or weaknesses of the portrait. Let's just agree that its merits will be discussed here, in this house, and nowhere else. You know perfectly well, Gregory, that you'd have to leave politics if that picture was in the Archibald. You've worked too hard to risk that. You've always said public life was the best way to make a difference. You didn't say anything about pubic life.'

As soon as she said this, Margaret cursed what she knew to be a tendency of hers to trivialise matters just to nail a joke. Gregory, inured to this tendency in his mother, having grown up with it, put his glass down and got to his feet. Margaret assessed his mood as pompous. Pompous usually referred to behaviour, but Gregory, especially during the difficult teenage years, managed to lend this quality to his moods.

'We're talking about a work of art,' he said. 'I haven't been caught having sex with some prostitute, or worse, someone from the opposition. I hope this picture does provoke discussion and controversy. Isn't that what art is supposed to do?'

'Why couldn't you have been painted in that lovely new suit of yours, the one you wore to the opening of that tram stop or whatever it was?'

'It was a major transport hub, and I didn't want to be painted in a suit, because I'd look like every other politician who's had his portrait painted, and that's precisely what I didn't want. And I also didn't want to be wearing casual clothes like a cut-rate, boorish uncle at a barbecue. Politics for me means leading by example. It means taking risks. If I wanted to cravenly pander to philistinism and general ignorance, I'd be on the other side.'

Phoebe, who'd been standing all this time, perched herself on the arm of the sofa on which Margaret was sitting.

'Controversy,' she said, 'is precisely what Sophie White wants. Good for her career, disastrous for yours.'

Gregory was exasperated, but he'd learned that he was poor at expressing exasperation. Somehow it always registered as a small, mean emotion, no matter how deep it ran. To counter this, he tended to exaggerate it, to try to make it read as big. He'd come to overlay many of his emotions with this theatrical element, so that genuine feelings had a habit of looking phoney. It was one of the things about her husband that Phoebe found less than endearing. Now, he placed his hands on his hips and expelled an exaggerated sigh.

'Look,' he said, 'the decision was essentially mine. I was paying, and I was calling the shots. I took guidance from Sophie White — she filled me in on a lot of the history of the Archibald — but what is hanging on the wall in there is what *I* wanted.'

'You haven't said how much that thing has cost us.'

Gregory thought about revealing this, but changed his mind. The money hadn't come out of their shared account. He'd tell Phoebe later, in private. There was no reason why his mother needed to know, and no reason why he should endure her inevitable gasps of disbelief. As a distraction, he asked, 'Another gin, Mum? You seem to have knocked that one back.'

'Well I like to hurry the first one down. It's important to have a good foundation to build on. Are you having another, Phoebe?'

'I've barely touched the one I've got.'

'Gregory?'

'No, I won't. I don't want to be even slightly bibulous when Phoebe's mum gets here.'

'Oh God. Is Joyce coming?' She held out her glass. 'Just fill it to the top with gin.'

Over many years of contemplation and inner struggle, Joyce Milford had become quietly reconciled to the fact that Phoebe was destined for eternal damnation in the bowels of hell. On her bedroom wall, facing her so that it was the last thing she saw at night, and the first thing she saw in the morning, was a large, high-quality print of Hieronymus Bosch's *The Last Judgement*. Bosch's vision of hell, with its grotesque monsters and writhing, broken, tortured bodies of the damned, was a source of comfort. She didn't entirely approve of the nudity, but hell was unarguably the place where it belonged. Years of staring at the painting — and each time she looked closely, she discovered some new, small horror — hadn't dulled her to the bleak power of Bosch's vision. The thought of Phoebe being pulled apart, or raped, or both, by some hideous fiend had ceased to bother her. She took a practical approach to Phoebe's inevitable descent into hell. Phoebe was an adult. She could make her own decisions. There was only so much a mother could do. If she wanted to walk, open-eyed, into hell's maw, that was her lookout.

Phoebe had telephoned her mother the previous day and had invited her to afternoon tea. She'd been mysterious about the reason and had said that she and Gregory simply wanted to catch up and that they did have a bit of news to impart. If the news was that Phoebe had finally found Jesus, the visit would be worthwhile. Any news other than this must be of minimal interest.

Still, Joyce was nothing if not a vessel of Christian charity, and so she'd accepted the invitation, despite the fact that she had no time at all for Gregory Buchanan. She found him obsequious — a charge that would have horrified him — and although he'd never said so, she knew that he was an atheist. There were many things about him that she disliked, but his atheism was chief among them. It was what he had in common with Phoebe, of course.

The evening after she first met him, she found his avatar there in the Bosch painting, or at any rate she found the figure that she liked to imagine was him. There was a trio of naked men, impaled on a tree, and she'd nominated Gregory as the one pinned upright, with a branch spike emerging through his genitals. She'd been known to go up to the painting and say 'Good morning, Gregory' to the writhing figure. This didn't seem mean to her. It was simply a projection of God's justice, and justice might be hard, but never mean. Besides, Joyce had a mission. Gregory wasn't the only one who could play at politics.

Before telephoning for the taxi that would take her to Phoebe and Gregory's house, she gathered together a sheaf of papers and ran her eye over the pages. Just looking at it gave her a sense of achievement, which she was quick to suppress in case it swelled into the vanity of self-congratulation. Somewhere in Bosch's crowded landscape, someone was being punished for committing the sin of pride. Joyce was sure of this. She put her papers in her large handbag, and when the taxi barped its horn, she leaned in close to the Bosch and tapped on the little Gregory figure.

'You're not in purgatory, you fool. You're pinned there for eternity. Welcome to hell.' She smiled and snapped her handbag shut.

The mention of Joyce's impending arrival had prompted Phoebe to apologise for springing this news on Margaret.

'I should have forewarned you.'

Gregory, predictably, leapt to his mother-in-law's defence and told Phoebe that he thought she was being unkind. This rankled with Phoebe, particularly as she had told Gregory on numerous occasions that whatever her mother's Christian pretensions, she was the unkindest person Phoebe had ever known. For the umpteenth time, she said, 'I don't know why you persist in claiming that you like her, especially when you know perfectly well that she doesn't just disapprove of you, she actively dislikes you.'

'Well I just don't think that's true.'

There wasn't a great deal of conviction in Gregory's voice. He didn't understand Phoebe's relationship with her mother, and if he were strapped to a chair and injected with sodium pentothal, he'd reveal that Joyce Milford frightened and intimidated him. He was never able to achieve Phoebe's calm detachment from Joyce's religious ravings. They were so hot and fierce that he shrank back from them; he never rose to the challenge of arguing with her. He supposed that Phoebe loved her mother and that Joyce loved Phoebe, because mothers and daughters loved each other, didn't they? Phoebe claimed that her mother's love was conditional on her being born again, and until that day it was held, or withheld, in a kind of suspended animation.

As Margaret sipped her second gin, both Phoebe and Gregory went into the kitchen to put the afternoon tea together. She got up from the sofa and returned to the dining room, where she examined the portrait once again. She shook her head and said to no one, 'Why?' She'd always assumed that Gregory shared her secret conservative streak, but this astonishing demonstration of exhibitionism put the tin hat on that idea. She couldn't even imagine Sally consenting to be painted like this, and Sally was a lesbian. Not that lesbians had a predilection for nude portraiture, but Margaret had, after all, discovered that her daughter was gay when she'd turned on the television, several years ago now, to see Sally riding topless among the Dykes on Bikes in the Sydney Mardi Gras parade. When Sally arrived home a few days later, Margaret said, 'I saw your breasts on telly a couple of nights ago, and so did half of Australia.'

Sally, who'd been dreading outing herself to her mother, rose to the occasion and said, 'How did they look?' Margaret was disarmed, and the difficult conversation turned out not to be difficult at all. Indeed, Margaret's usually disciplined nosiness had given way to questions that Sally found intrusive rather than supportive. In keeping with her public liberalism, Margaret declared herself an LGBTQIA ally and began ruining Sally's gay-pride marches by marching in them as well.

While looking at the portrait, Margaret reflected that Gregory must have inherited more genes from her than from his father, whose body had never looked like this, not even in the early days of their marriage — and by the time of his relatively early death, every entropic destiny written into his DNA had played itself out. She missed him. She missed him terribly.

When Phoebe returned to the dining room, she was surprised to find Margaret dabbing tears from her eyes.

'It's awful, but it's not that bad,' Phoebe said.

'I was just thinking of Barry, and how much I miss him.'

'Does Gregory look a lot like his father?'

'Oh lord no. Not in the least. Gregory's an Adonis compared to Barry. My kids both got lucky. They inherited their father's brains, but not his looks. Sometimes it just hits me what a shame it is that Barry isn't here to see how well Gregory and Sally turned out.'

'What would he have said about this portrait?'

Margaret thought for a moment, took a sip of her drink, and said, 'Oh, Barry would have been on Gregory's side. Gregory might have got this exhibitionist streak from him.'

'Was Barry a nudist?'

'Oh no, no, no. More of a free thinker. I'd give anything to have him back.'

She smiled at Phoebe, and there was something so heartbreaking in that smile that Phoebe blurted out, 'I'm pregnant.'

Margaret's smile went from melancholic to radiant.

'Oh, Phoebe, how wonderful!'

'I've spoilt the surprise now. I was supposed to wait until Mum and Sally were here as well.'

'I felt there was something going on. You've barely touched your drink.'

They returned to the living room, and Phoebe called Gregory from the kitchen.

'Margaret knows,' she said.

'I guessed, darling, so don't be cross with Phoebe. I figured you hadn't summoned us all here just to see your cock. I'm sorry, that's the gin talking.'

Phoebe laughed. Gregory didn't. Margaret hurried on.

'When is she due?'

'We don't know the sex,' said Phoebe. 'We don't want to know.'

'I was just being optimistic. A grandchild to indulge

and corrupt. I'm so happy for you. It really is the most glorious news.'

'The baby is due in November. You don't think that tiny sip of gin has done any damage, do you? It was ninety-nine per cent tonic.'

Margaret snorted. 'Don't be silly.'

'It's just such a responsibility being pregnant. Fetal alcohol syndrome, toxoplasmosis, listeria, coliform bacteria. My vocabulary is getting better, but I feel under siege.'

'Will Joyce be pleased, do you think?'

'She'll be thrilled,' Gregory said. 'Of course she'll be thrilled. Honestly, what a question! She's Phoebe's mother, for God's sake, not Grendel's.'

Phoebe was unconvinced yet again by Gregory's advocacy on behalf of her mother.

'Whatever excitement she feels will be tempered by her belief that this is a soul in peril.'

Gregory was about to say something, but Phoebe spoke firmly ahead of his interruption.

'*And* your portrait isn't going to inspire confidence in us as God-fearing parents, is it?'

Her smile was the smile of someone who felt sure she'd just made a telling point.

'You don't give your mother much credit, Phoebe,' Gregory said, rather weakly.

'She exhausted her credit years ago.'

Margaret could see that this might easily slide into

unpleasant and pointless bickering, and it would be the sort of bickering that had no freshness to it. This was stale soil, tilled too often and offering only familiar sourness.

'Your sister is on a diet,' she said breezily, as if this were a conversational gambit so compelling that pursuing it would be irresistible to any listener. Phoebe and Gregory looked at her, uncertain what was required of them. There was an awkward pause, which Margaret took to be evidence that the argument had been successfully short-circuited. She didn't allow the pause to stand.

'Sally's gone fitness mad. She barely eats. She thinks lip balm is a food group, and she cycles everywhere. I'm sure it's marvellous. She's reducing her carbon footprint to a scuff mark. She's riding here and it's a forty-kilometre round trip.'

'Well good for her,' Gregory said. 'Not that she needed to lose weight.'

'All that lycra, though. It's a recipe for a yeast infection.'

'I hope you're encouraging her, Mum.'

'Of course I'm encouraging her — mainly to be on the lookout for a yeast infection.'

With the threat of the small, domestic argument averted, Margaret put her drink down and excused herself. She knew her way around the house, so didn't need directions to the downstairs toilet.

'You know, Phoebe,' said Gregory, 'I don't think the whole family has ever been in the same room together. You, me, Joyce, Mum, and Sally. We've been married for seven years and this will be the first time.'

'There was our wedding.'

'Yes, but there were other people around.'

'When Mum and Sally find out why they're here, they'll all be on their best behaviour, although Mum doesn't really have a best behaviour. She just has behaviour.'

Phoebe's mention of their wedding brought that occasion back to Gregory. It had been mostly a joyous event, but even he couldn't expunge from his memory the embarrassing spectacle of Joyce Milford loudly declaring that she would stay outside and pray for the duration of the service rather than soil her retinas with the idolatrous statuary that stood about within. Phoebe had warned Gregory that this would happen. He'd believed that Joyce would relax her beliefs enough to see her daughter married. He'd been wrong.

The recollection of Joyce on her knees on the concrete, in a light drizzle, like some mendicant pilgrim, her open Bible soaking up the rain, made Gregory think that her reaction to his portrait might be as predictable as Phoebe insisted it would be. He tried telling himself that she might surprise them all, but the image of her resolutely refusing to get up off her knees as the congregation left the church and flowed around her came back to him, and he knew that Joyce wasn't in the business of surprising anyone. Her great shield was, as Phoebe said, her inability to be embarrassed by her own actions. She experienced self-righteous indignation, feverish incredulity, but never embarrassment.

'What are you thinking?' Phoebe asked.

'It's not so much what I was thinking, but what I was hoping. I was hoping, vainly probably, that Joyce might see my portrait's artistic merit.'

Phoebe laughed.

'What she'll see is *you* naked, and I'm quietly confident that you'll be the first naked man she's ever seen.'

'She was married to your father for twenty years. Surely …'

'You never met my father. If you had, you'd have noticed the air of disappointment that hung around him.'

When Margaret returned to the living room, she found Phoebe and Gregory engaged in equable and unheated conversation. She thought it was safe to satisfy her curiosity about the extent of Joyce's Christian beliefs.

'Before your mother gets here, Phoebe, can I ask you how conservative her views really are? I mean, she produced you and you're not religious at all. Or are you? Perhaps I'm speaking out of turn.'

'What would we do without your blithe indifference to people's feelings, Mum?'

Margaret had retrieved her drink and took a generous sip.

'I just don't want to say the wrong thing. I don't want to embarrass or offend Phoebe. I don't mind offending you, darling. That's why we have children. It's one of the small compensations for childbirth. My bladder was never the same after I had you. Oh, I'm so sorry, Phoebe. I don't mean to alarm you.'

Phoebe smiled.

'Oh, don't worry, Margaret. I didn't even know I had a pelvic floor until I got pregnant. Now it's the main focus of my exercise regime.'

'Wouldn't it be nice if men suffered sympathetic incontinence?'

'Sympathetic anything, really.'

Gregory looked mildly stung.

'I'm only kidding,' Phoebe said.

Margaret stored this exchange away for later consideration. Had her son's performance of sympathy in the political arena dulled his capacity to experience the real thing? Had Gregory ever uttered the empty phrase 'thoughts and prayers', she wondered. She hoped not. She'd think about it afterwards. For now, she wanted to get some grasp on what she thought of as Joyce Milford's mental illness.

'Tell me about Joyce.'

'My mother believes in the literal truth of the Bible, and I mean the whole box and dice. But you know this already, Margaret.'

'I've never really taken it in. Go on.'

'She believes the world is six thousand years old. I mean, she really, really believes this. She's a proper, hardcore creationist.'

'She has little eccentricities,' Gregory said. 'Don't we all?'

Phoebe flared with irritation.

'Religious fanaticism isn't a little eccentricity. It's a destructive, obliterating ugliness.'

Gregory raised his hands in defeat. He was annoyed with his mother for raising the subject.

'I think we should talk about something else,' he said.

'A creationist,' Margaret said, unwilling to drop the matter. 'I had dinner with a creationist, a while ago now. It was after your father died. I suppose it was a kind of date. A deeply misguided friend set it up. It was all going okay until dessert, when the matter of faith popped up, and when he wondered if I shared his view that he was made in God's image. Apparently God is bald, slightly overweight, and has an overbite that ought to have been seen to in childhood.'

She took another sip of her drink.

'I don't think creationists would be very good at sex, do you? Joyless and functional.'

'Mum, please.'

'I'm still orgasmic, Gregory. Very much so.'

Gregory put his hands over his ears.

'No one should ever have to hear his mother say

"orgasmic", especially when she's talking about herself.'

'It's only a word. I've just been obliged to stare at your penis. I think that pretty much trumps anything I might *say*.'

Phoebe stood up and returned to the portrait. She was hoping that in the intervening few minutes something in her aesthetic understanding of the world might have shifted. Perhaps Gregory's spirited defence of the picture might have changed her view of it without her realising it. She was disappointed. There it hung in all its swaggering ghastliness. Gregory turned his head so that he could see her, although he couldn't see the painting. She looked back at him.

'This is *not* going in the Archibald. The only travelling it's doing is upstairs into the spare bedroom. Now might be a good time, before Mum gets here. I think we can agree what her reaction will be, and you've put me in the position of having to concur with my mother on something. That is possibly the most egregious consequence of this project of yours.'

Before Gregory could reply, Margaret cut across him.

'Oh no, Phoebe, not the spare room. That's where I sleep when I stay here. I wouldn't sleep a wink.'

'Well it's not going in our bedroom.'

'I think this is what they call a problem picture.'

Gregory said, calmly, 'It's staying where it is, thank you very much.'

Phoebe dismissed this with a wave of her hand.

'People eat in here, darling. I don't think this painting goes with food, do you, seriously?'

Gregory stood up and took Margaret's glass, assuming that she'd require a top up. She relinquished the glass with a smile. As he walked to the kitchen, he said, raising his voice as he moved out of sight, 'I can't believe the two of you. This is not a piece of amateur rubbish. It's by one of this country's leading artists at the top of her form. That portrait might just be a masterpiece.'

Phoebe caught Margaret's eye and shook her head.

Gregory continued. 'History is littered with people rejecting masterpieces in favour of dull, safe pictures. Safe is for the academy. Safe isn't in my political vocabulary. Whoever made a difference by being safe?'

He returned to the living room and gave Margaret her drink.

'Give me the refusés every time,' he said. 'That's where art really happens.'

'When Mum gets here, she'll give you some idea what refusé means.'

'I don't want to defend Joyce — I know how much you hate that — but in some ways you have to admire her commitment to her faith.'

'That's like admiring someone's determination to kill people in the middle of a psychotic episode.' Was that going too far? She crossed to Gregory, put her arms around him, and kissed him on the lips. 'Please stop auditioning for the role of my mother's favourite son-in-law. You're her *only* son-in-law, you don't believe in God, and you're on the wrong side of politics. My mother thinks you're evil. She prays for you, in a half-hearted sort of way I imagine. She thinks hell is under-populated.'

Gregory sighed and kissed Phoebe's forehead.

'All right. This is a happy occasion.' He looked pointedly at his mother. 'Please don't get into an argument with Joyce about religion. You're not going to change her views, and what does it matter what she thinks?'

'It's always the sane who have to accommodate the crazy people. I'm not going to attack Joyce, but if she says something outrageous, especially about you, I'm not going to just let it pass.'

'She will say something outrageous,' Phoebe said. 'It's the most reliable thing about her.'

Just as she said this, the doorbell rang.

'That and her punctuality.'

While Gregory answered the door, Margaret asked Phoebe very quietly if her relationship with her mother qualified as an estrangement. Before Phoebe could answer, Gregory returned.

'That's the taxi driver at the door. Joyce is refusing to get out of his taxi. She thinks she's being overcharged.'

Phoebe uttered a theatrical sigh.

'Is the taxi driver an Indian man?'

'Yes he is.'

'Mum thinks you're allowed to bargain if the other person isn't white.'

'Let Gregory sort it out,' Margaret said. 'He's the minister for transport.'

'Helpful as always, Mum. I'll just pay the man.'

Gregory echoed Phoebe's theatrical sigh and left the room.

'What were we talking about, Margaret? Sorry, Mum has done what she always does. She likes to put everyone on edge, and she can do it at any distance. It's all about control.'

'Gregory's portrait will put her off her stroke.'

'That's the one positive thing about that bloody picture — it will appal my mother all the way down to the subatomic level. Now, what were we saying?'

Margaret might not have pursued such an intimate line of inquiry, but emboldened by gin she repeated her question about Phoebe's relationship with her mother, prefacing it this time with the hope that it wasn't an intrusive or unwelcome question.

'Oh, that's quite all right,' Phoebe said. 'I'm happy to talk about it. It's a cheap form of cognitive behavioural therapy. The thing is, we're generally civil to each other, but we disagree about almost everything, and especially about the fundamental things like how to lead a good life. It sounds horrible to say it, but the truth is she blighted my childhood. She told me awful things, horrifying things. Everything was a dire warning. It was like being inside the Bosch painting she has on her bedroom wall. There was something in me, though, some natural immunity against the poison. I knew Noah's ark was bullshit. Where were the emus? Where were the koalas? Where were the dung beetles? And what kind of genetic nightmare would result from generations of mammalian incest? I understood at an unnaturally early age that my mother was a stupid person, and I spent my childhood accommodating this sad fact.'

Margaret reached out and squeezed Phoebe's hand. Phoebe smiled.

'My father died when I was very young. I think now he must have wanted to.'

Margaret suddenly felt that she might have inadvertently encouraged Phoebe to overshare. Thinking that she ought to offer something in return, she said, 'Gregory and I don't always see eye to eye, and I frequently row with Sally. She can be very exasperating. It's always over silly things, though.'

'Yes, but you actually like your children. My mother doesn't like me. I'm not upset about it. It's an inescapable fact. She'd be appalled to hear me say it, of course, and deny it, but she doesn't really like anyone. She pretends to. It's all part of being a good Christian woman, but like all her type she's not fuelled by love, but by hatred and malice. It's all dressed up as moral rectitude, but really it's just hatred. I got so used to her railing against the world that I was numbed to it. The worst of it was, it did damage me, and made me suspicious of everyone. Gregory rescued me from that. He was so optimistic and passionate, and heartbreakingly naive.'

Phoebe paused.

'Your son is the only man I've ever loved, Margaret.'

This declaration took Margaret so by surprise that her eyes welled with tears. It was Phoebe's turn to reach out and squeeze Margaret's hand.

'He's not perfect. He has his foibles, and I'm afraid one of them is vanity, and he's susceptible to flattery.'

Margaret bridled a little at this, as though it represented a failure of mothering.

'Is he?'

'Look at his portrait. Gregory can't see that this Sophie White person has flattered him blind. That's a confusing notion because there's nothing flattering about the way she's painted his face. Somehow he's willfully blind to it. I hate the way she's exploited his vanity by convincing him that it's a brave moment in Australian politics.'

'Is it well painted do you think?'

'Regrettably, yes. It's an accomplished piece of work. I'll grant her that. It's very lifelike, and yet it isn't.

She's made him look venal and grasping and viciously ambitious, and he isn't any of those things.'

'I'll have to have another look. I can't say I saw those things, but I was a bit distracted by the overall effect.'

The sound of the front door closing signalled the imminent entrance of Joyce. When she came into the room, her eyes fell immediately on Margaret. They rested there for longer than was strictly necessary before she spoke.

'Taxi drivers must think I came down in the last shower.'

She was soberly dressed in brown. Her iron-grey hair was cut as it had been for as long as Phoebe could remember. It was what might be called a serviceable haircut, one that required minimal attention in the mirror. Joyce didn't care for mirrors, not because she didn't like what she saw in them, but because they represented an occasion for vanity, and vanity was the besetting ill of the twenty-first century. Whenever Joyce left the house, she did so without primping and preening first. To be clean and presentable was her aim, with no features enhanced or disguised by make-up. To imply that the face God gave you required an adjustment was an affront to His creation. She sometimes, in moments of weakness, wished that the Lord hadn't been quite so generous with the breasts He'd given her. They were uncomfortable and drew unwelcome eyes. After such moments, she did severe penance. Her bosom was part of God's plan, and it was a burden she was obliged to carry.

'It's good to see you, Mum. You know Margaret, of course. Gregory's mother.'

Joyce now felt she had permission to take in Margaret from head to foot. Too much make-up. High-maintenance hair.

'Oh yes. The last time we met, you were terribly drunk. You probably don't remember much about it. Alcohol-related memory loss is quite common among heavy drinkers, I believe.'

Margaret hadn't been prepared for such a strong opening volley from Joyce, but she rallied.

'I remember everything about it with dispiriting clarity, Joyce.'

Joyce produced what might technically be called a smile, but it had no warmth.

'You called me a moron,' she said. 'Apparently it was something I said.'

'I think it was just that you said something.'

Joyce reproduced an exact copy of her joyless smile, although perhaps it wasn't quite an exact copy, because she tried to imbue it with a sense that her overriding feeling about Margaret was pity. Margaret returned the smile and for her part hoped that Joyce would read the contempt in it.

'Almost everyone's here,' Phoebe said, in an attempt to impose normalcy. 'We're just waiting for Sally.'

'Sally is my daughter,' Margaret said.

Not wishing to acknowledge Margaret's role in the creation of Sally, Joyce said, 'I don't think I knew that Gregory had a sister.'

'Yes you did, Mum. I've mentioned Sally to you many times.'

'She's a lesbian,' Margaret said. 'Perhaps if you don't remember her, you'll remember her outstanding immorality.'

Joyce wasn't to be drawn, and she was relieved of expending any energy on her wintry smile by Gregory's return.

'That's all taken care of. He's not going to press charges.'

Phoebe's mouth opened in surprise. Pre-empting any utterance, Joyce said, 'What a ridiculous carry-on. I was gesturing and knocked one of those hideous pagan idols off the dashboard. It was half-elephant, if you please. What kind of person worships an elephant? The trunk snapped, and the silly man got it into his head that I'd done it on purpose.'

'And had you done it on purpose, Mum?'

'As far as I'm concerned, it was an accident, but I can't be responsible if the Holy Spirit directs my hand against something that offends him.'

'The Holy Spirit?' Margaret said. 'That's a pigeon, isn't it? As opposed to an elephant, I mean.'

Gregory glared meaningfully at his mother.

'I'll make some tea,' Phoebe said, and left the room.

There was an awkward silence.

Joyce looked around the room, deliberately avoiding Margaret's eye by scanning over her head. Perhaps she was looking for some evidence that the household had assumed Christian values since her last visit. In her own house, such evidence wasn't to be found in lurid, framed pictures of the Sacred Heart, or crucifixes depending from hooks. She disapproved of such paraphernalia, finding them as offensive in their way as what she considered the extravagant grotesqueries of other faiths. You would know where Joyce stood if you were invited into her house by the books on her shelves and the framed passages from the Bible. These weren't soft, new-age aphorisms. They were terrifying warnings about the consequences of sinfulness.

Gregory said, 'Have you been well, Joyce?'

'I have a robust constitution, which I put at the service of the Lord.' She turned to Gregory and gave him her full attention.

'Gregory, perhaps Phoebe told you, I'm giving the keynote speech at a conference on Christian education next week. My researches have been most enlightening, and alarming. Were you aware that Christian doctrine is not compulsory in state primary schools? You probably think that's perfectly all right. Well it isn't, Gregory, it isn't. There are children out there who think that Jesus is the Brazilian kiddie down the road. It's heartbreaking.'

Gregory, aware that his mother was poised to say something, rather hurriedly said, 'Christian doctrine can't be made compulsory, Joyce, not in state schools. That's why they're called state schools.'

Joyce emitted a sound that resembled a harrumph and said firmly, 'Can't isn't in my vocabulary.'

'Take out the apostrophe and it is,' Margaret said.

Joyce, in keeping with her general policy with regards to Margaret, ignored her. She reached into her voluminous carry bag and pulled forth a piece of paper.

'I was going to do this later, but I might as well give it to you while we're on the subject. I believe in striking while the iron is hot. This, Gregory, is a petition. It has fifty, *fifty* signatures on it demanding the immediate introduction of compulsory Christian doctrine in all schools. *All* schools, primary and secondary. You are to take this to the premier and warn her that she stands in peril of losing these votes.'

She waved the document at Gregory and he reluctantly took it, knowing that none of the people whose names were appended to it had voted for Louisa Wetherly in the last election, and that they had no intention of voting for her in the next one.

'Fifty signatures do not a multitude make,' Margaret said.

Looking at Gregory, not at Margaret, Joyce said, 'We are a moral force. We are a whirlwind.'

'Windy certainly,' Margaret said.

Phoebe came back into the room, carrying the tea things.

'Now, when you present this to the premier …'

Phoebe interrupted her. Joyce's voice had carried into the kitchen.

'Gregory can't present your petition, Mum.'

'Why not?'

'For a start, he doesn't support it.'

'But it's common sense. What type of person doesn't support common sense?'

Regretting it, even as she asked the question, Phoebe said, 'What is it exactly that you're petitioning for, Mum? The details.'

'I've already said. You must have heard me from the kitchen. Christian doctrine must be compulsory in all schools.'

'Even Islamic schools?' Margaret asked.

'Especially Islamic schools.'

'That's just laughable, Mum.'

Gregory, who'd been reading Joyce's petition — not because he was interested but because it excused him from conversation — couldn't contain a small gasp.

'Is something wrong, Gregory?' Joyce said, with no hint of concern.

'You want creationism taught in the science curriculum.'

'Which is where it belongs. The moral decline in this country is terrifying. Terrifying.'

Joyce had a way of repeating her words as if repetition made them true.

'We're being buried under an avalanche of filth and misinformation. Take a walk down any street and what do you see? Girls dressed like strumpets on the Rue Pigalle, and boys half-naked and foul-mouthed. What happened to decorum and decency? I'll tell you what happened. Science. Science. People deporting themselves like trollops and pimps is the tip of the iceberg. What's being pushed into their heads is rotting them from the inside out. Christian modesty, Christian modesty must be reasserted.'

'Gregory's had his portrait painted,' Margaret said, and smiled with pleasure at such a satisfyingly placed non sequitur. Joyce, who thought portraits were a symptom of corrosive vanity, said, 'An official portrait is a little premature, isn't it, Gregory?'

Gregory narrowed his eyes at his mother, who opened hers wide in a display of mock innocence.

'It's not really an official portrait, Joyce. I commissioned it.'

'Ah,' Joyce said, managing to convey in that single expression that all her suspicions and reservations about Gregory's character were now confirmed.

'It's not just a portrait, Joyce. It's a work of art.'

'And where is this work of art?' The little sneer that attended the words 'work of art' escaped no one. Although he wouldn't admit it, Gregory's last little hope that Joyce might be beguiled by Sophie White's skill had deserted him.

'It's on the wall in the dining room,' he said.

'Finish your tea first, Mum, and have a biscuit. I made them.'

'Perhaps just the tea,' Joyce said. 'Just the tea.'

'I'd have a biscuit if I were you,' Phoebe said. 'You're going to need the sugar.'

'If you've got any heroin lying around, that might be better,' Margaret said.

This remark made no sense to Joyce, but she filed it away as evidence that Margaret might be both a high-functioning alcoholic and a drug addict.

'I at least hope that it looks like you and isn't one of those frightful modern things. Only incompetent artists peddle the notion that a likeness isn't important.'

'Oh no,' Margaret said. 'It's a very good likeness.' In imitation of Joyce, she added, 'A very good likeness.'

Joyce, who thought too much fuss was being made of an inconsequential act of self-promotion, took her cup of tea and went into the dining room. Gregory, Phoebe, and Margaret exchanged looks. Margaret was hoping for the cliché of a dropped teacup and saucer. There was silence. No one moved. Joyce returned to the living room. Her face had lost none of its colour, so she wasn't suffering from shock. She put her cup and saucer down and stood very still. She closed her eyes as if in prayer.

'Are you going to say something, Mum?'

With unwavering calm and keeping her eyes closed, she said, 'What is there to say, Phoebe? I have stared wickedness in the face.'

'And not just in the face,' Margaret said.

Casting a knowing look at Gregory, Phoebe said, 'So you weren't impressed by the sfumato?'

'I don't know what that word means. It sounds foreign and lewd.'

With tone-deaf irrelevance, Gregory said, 'It's the play of tonal values, the softening of transitions between them.'

Joyce opened her eyes and turned them on Gregory.

'It's pornography. I can barely bring myself to look at you. I feel soiled. Violated. It's obscene, disgusting, horrific, an abomination. You should take it down at once and burn it, reduce it to ashes. Ashes.'

'So you wouldn't be in favour of it hanging in the Archibald, then?' Phoebe said.

'It pollutes the air I breathe. It pollutes the air we all breathe.'

This was too much, even for Gregory.

'I'm sorry, Joyce, but I think you're overreacting.'

Joyce breathed in and exhaled quickly, perhaps remembering what she'd just said. She turned her body to face Gregory, but kept her face resolutely in profile.

'Do not speak to me. You have thrown filth in my face. Ordure. Ordure. I can't say I'm disappointed in you, because I've always known what lurks behind your polite facade. You are a whited sepulchre. I've always said so.'

'That's my son you're disparaging, Joyce.'

'The apple doesn't fall far from the tree. Your son is a loathsome pornographer.'

Margaret put her hands on her hips, a gesture familiar to Gregory from his youth. It was always the prelude to a dressing down.

'It's just a painting, Joyce. Not one that would go with most people's furnishings, I grant you, but it's a very long way from pornography. If you call it an abomination, what language are you left with to describe the real horrors in the world?'

Joyce looked at Margaret, and her granite-set features softened slightly into disbelief. She pointed at Gregory.

'He is brazenly naked!'

'I am *not* naked. I am nude. When I posed for Sophie White …'

Joyce gave every indication that she couldn't believe what she'd just heard.

'You paraded like *that* before a *woman*?'

'When I *posed* for Sophie White, I was naked. When you take your clothes off, you're naked. An artist transforms nakedness, elevates it to the nude. It becomes a cultural object. It has moral seriousness.'

'Moral!' Joyce's voice rose an octave.

'Yes. Moral.'

It had been a while since Phoebe had seen Gregory so energised by an argument.

'It's not me up there on the wall. It's a body transmuted. History won't care two figs who I was. What will survive will be Sophie White's rendering of the nude. It now sits within the long history of the nude in art.'

Even Gregory seemed aware that he'd slipped into embarrassing pomposity, and Phoebe didn't spare him.

'I don't know which is more ridiculous — Mum's Puritan nonsense or your art-theory twaddle. The point is, it's not going in the Archibald. That is all that matters.'

Joyce wasn't quite at the end of her outrage.

'I won't set foot here after today so long as that obscene object is on display. You've turned this house into a brothel, a great sink of lust and depravity.'

Margaret began laughing, which increased the tension in the room instead of dissipating it.

Gregory said, 'I'm sorry you feel this way, Joyce, but with the greatest respect, I think your position is wrong.'

'Respect! How dare you use that word? I'm surprised your tongue doesn't swell and blacken.'

Margaret, who'd never seen Joyce in full medieval umbrage, was delirious with delight. She was beginning to assemble some of her well-worn quotes to hurl at Joyce when the moment presented itself. Just now though, she left the field to Gregory, who, she thought, really ought to be more impressive.

'Every word spoken here makes me more determined to put my portrait in the Archibald Prize.'

'No,' Phoebe said. 'That is not happening.'

'It cost ten thousand dollars,' Gregory said, as if this sealed the argument in his favour.

Phoebe coughed in disbelief.

'What?'

'Wickedness upon wickedness!'

'After the Archibald, it will be worth twice that,' Gregory said. 'And within a few years, twice that again.'

'To whom?' Phoebe said. 'And even if that were true, your political career would be over.'

Joyce made a small movement as if she were about to head back to the dining room.

'It must be destroyed.'

Margaret, who was still hoping to direct a few Biblical-based darts at Joyce, decided that now was not the time. Instead she said, 'No one's going to destroy it, Joyce. We don't believe in destroying pictures, or burning books. Gregory's portrait ought not to hang in a public place, that's as much agreement as you'll get out of me — and I hasten to add that my reasons share nothing with yours. I can see it, Phoebe can see it, and for some inexplicable reason Gregory's blind to it, but a public showing of that picture would scuttle Gregory's political ambitions. The simple fact is that no one is going to step into a polling booth and vote for a premier, or a prime minister, whose genitals can be googled.'

'What rot,' Joyce said. 'It's perfectly all right to destroy a painting if it offends. Lady Churchill very sensibly destroyed an odious portrait of Sir Winston. It was her right, she owned it, and she exercised that right.'

'That was a notorious act of vandalism,' Gregory said. 'It was a Graham Sutherland portrait for God's sake.'

'Sir Winston loathed it. He thought it made him look like a toad.'

'He loathed it because it looked like him. Lady Churchill had form, of course. It wasn't the first portrait she'd destroyed. She ought to have been thrown into prison.'

Joyce sniffed. 'We don't throw people into prison for disposing of their own property in the way which suits them.'

'It was a barbarian act to exercise her right of ownership in that way. A civilised person would have distinguished between ownership and stewardship.'

'Hogwash. The only good thing to be said about it is that at least he had his clothes on.'

Gregory, knowing that he was on a hiding to nothing, said, 'Churchill was a nudist, as a matter of fact. The human body is not obscene, Joyce.'

'I'll think you'll find the Lord begs to differ … *and they knew that they were naked and they sewed fig leaves together and made themselves aprons.*'

'Not the most practical items of clothing,' Margaret said. Gregory could see his mother getting ready to launch a theological attack. There was a look of joyful expectancy on her face. He put his hands up.

'Please, can we not have an argument over the Bible?'

Just as he said this, his phone chirruped, a ring tone that Phoebe found extremely annoying, but which Gregory refused to change. Most of the time it wasn't an issue, but if Gregory's phone rang when they were in the middle of a small disagreement, it so irritated Phoebe that the disagreement often escalated into an argument. Gregory looked at his phone.

'It's Sophie White,' he said. 'I'm sorry, I need to take this. We're finalising the details about the Archibald entry. Just so you know.' He shot each of the women in the room a sharp little look of defiance. Each returned his look with her own expression of resolute distaste. He'd barely left the room when Phoebe's phone rang.

'Oh, please excuse me. This is work. We're in damage control over a client. Football player. Urinating in public. The usual thing.'

As Phoebe left the room, Joyce sighed, and in that sigh was an eloquent dismissal of her daughter's career. Public relations in the service of any enterprise other than spreading the word of God was despicable and disreputable. Joyce looked at the ceiling. Margaret looked at Joyce. She was wondering how to begin.

'You know, Joyce, I'm bewildered.'

Joyce lowered her eyes to look directly at Margaret.

'You'll get no argument from me on that score.'

Margaret acknowledged to herself that this opening gambit had been a misstep. It was a mistake to underestimate Joyce. She decided to be a little more head-on.

'I believe you think the world is six thousand years old.'

'I have no intention of discussing my beliefs with you, let alone defending them.'

'Why is that women pop up in the Bible mostly so that men can throw stones at them?'

'You're rambling. How much have you had to drink?'

Margaret looked at her empty glass. 'Not nearly enough.'

Joyce rummaged about in her bag. She was looking for nothing. It was simply a distraction from Margaret.

'Leviticus and Deuteronomy, Joyce. Leviticus and Deuteronomy. The two most inconvenient books in the Bible.'

'Don't cite scripture at me, Margaret.'

Joyce's tone signalled a shift in the nature of the conversation. She was no longer feigning boredom. There was a fierceness in her voice that Margaret responded to in kind.

'Citing scripture isn't your privilege alone, Joyce.'

'Scripture is a shield, not a weapon. If you're too blind or wicked to understand it and live by it, that's too bad for you.'

'Oh, I've read it, Joyce. Leviticus and Deuteronomy. The books of the law, with all their insane injunctions against the blind, the short-sighted, the lame, a flat nose, a broken hand, a crooked back, scabs, scurvy and dwarfism, and men who lose a testicle. Isn't it perverse that God would make you this way and then declare that you may not approach his altar because you are offensive to him? I believe we call that blaming the victim.'

'Drink up, Margaret.'

Margaret was feeling energised. This was a rare opportunity, and she didn't want to waste it. Only a very small part of her worried that she might end up spoiling Phoebe and Gregory's news.

'You can stand there, Joyce, as stolidly as you like, but how can you reconcile your belief in a just and merciful God with his notions on women and his unhealthy obsession with virginity?'

'Virginity is a precious gift, as a late, lamented prime minister quite rightly pointed out.'

'Oh yes. He ludicrously suggested the greatest gift his daughters could bring to a marriage was their virginity. Personally, a hymen seems like a crap present to me. It's one of those disappointing, single-use-only things. A much better present might be, I don't know, a house?'

Joyce summoned the energy to curl her lip.

'You find that distasteful?' Margaret said. 'How about God's solution to a husband discovering that his wife's hymen isn't intact? *Then they shall bring out the damsel to the door of her father's house and the men of the city shall stone her with stones, that she died.'*

This little recitation gave Margaret a great deal of pleasure. She believed that she'd spoken it well.

'I don't expect to move you, Joyce, with any of this, but you know what really makes me angry at people like you? It's how your literal reading endorses, by its very literalness, God's view of rape. *If a damsel that is a virgin be betrothed unto a husband, and a man find her in the city, and lie with her, then ye shall bring them both out unto the gate of that city, and ye shall stone them with stones that they die; the damsel because she cried not, being in the city, and the man because he has humbled his neighbour's wife: so thou shalt put away evil from among you.'*

Margaret paused, satisfied with the fluency of her recitation and rather pleased that she'd remembered it verbatim. She then experienced an unexpected rush of rage that took her by surprise.

'How can you endorse that crap!'

Joyce, the pink blush in her cheek betraying her anger now, said, 'This is tiresome, Margaret. You've gone to all the trouble of learning a few verses and think you've proved some point or other.'

'*He that is wounded in the stones or have his privy member cut off shall not enter into the congregation of the Lord.'*

'The laws that you are cherrypicking were for a

particular time, and were for the Jews. The death and resurrection of our Lord provided the world with new salvation and release from ancient precepts.'

'Even if I accept that they were God's laws for his chosen people, why should we shrug off the consequences for Jewish women, Jewish dwarfs, and Jewish men with one ball?'

'I do not presume to know the mind of God. I don't even presume to know yours, although you're unable to return that courtesy.'

'I don't presume to know his mind either, otherwise I might be able to come up with some explanation for his whole-hearted approval of slavery.'

With as much condescension as she could muster, Joyce said, 'I'm not a theologian, Margaret. I'm a simple person of faith.'

'I sometimes think all the simple people of faith have only read the Cecil B. DeMille bits of the Bible, and have somehow missed that God is just a horrifying cohort of men masquerading as him. If there is a God, he can't be the dim, irrational figure who forbids tattoos but insists on circumcision.'

Joyce, tamping down a more serious fulmination that was threatening to explode, said, 'Now you've strayed into blasphemy, and that offends me, and it offends God.'

'You think he's actively listening to us?'

'He hears the most secret murmurings of your heart.'

The doorbell rang as Joyce was making small movements indicating her intention to leave. She'd delivered her petition and had no desire to talk further with a woman she considered beyond redemption. Phoebe came in with her phone still to her ear.

'I'll get the door,' she said, and noticed that her mother was standing in an attitude of rigid determination.

'I'm leaving, Phoebe. After you've answered the door, telephone for a taxi.'

'We'll talk about this in a moment, Mum.'

Joyce, looking down on Margaret, said, with icy clarity, 'I see now why Gregory has no moral compass. I hope you appreciate the patience with which I've endured your unprovoked attack. Clearly you wanted to get it out of your system. It sounded horribly rehearsed. I think perhaps even over-rehearsed. I have nothing to say to you. Did you think you could shake my faith? You might as well stamp your foot and hope to make a mountain tremble.'

Phoebe came into the room, her phone call now concluded, ahead of Sally Buchanan, Gregory's sister. Sally was a little red in the face, having ridden a considerable distance. She was dressed in bright lycra, and her cycling shoes clattered noisily on the wooden floor as she walked. She was smiling broadly. Sally was always smiling broadly, which irritated Margaret no end. She found her daughter's general positivity exhausting. Phoebe, choosing to ignore for the moment whatever had happened between Joyce and Margaret in her absence, said, 'Sally, this is my mother, Joyce. I don't think you've met.'

'No, we haven't,' said Sally, beaming. 'But I saw you at the wedding, I think. How do you do?'

She extended her hand. Joyce shook it without hesitation, a gesture that had the peculiar effect of enraging Margaret.

'I'm quite well, thank you. I was just leaving.'

'No, Mum, you can't leave yet. We asked you here for a reason.'

'I've seen the reason.'

There was a meanness in Margaret that bubbled to the surface. She didn't want Sally having any positive feelings about Joyce, and she was prepared to sabotage the meeting to ensure this.

'Sally, darling,' she said. 'Joyce here believes that you are the incarnation of evil.'

Sally, who despite her smile had taken the temperature of the room as she'd entered, and knew about Joyce from conversations she'd had with Phoebe, and had a good notion what Joyce thought of her sexuality, nevertheless opted for displacement.

'Well, not everyone likes lycra. I have brought a change of clothes.'

The remark went unappreciated. Joyce turned to Margaret and with real fierceness said, 'This is insupportable! How dare you say such a thing! How dare you speak for me!'

Gregory, who was about to come back into the room, was given pause by the real anger in Joyce's voice. He knew himself well enough to know that his supposed toleration of Joyce's rigid religious views was born of fear, not respect. He was afraid of Joyce. That's what it came down to. He'd been described more than once in the press as a conciliation politician, and he'd been pleased with that description. Phoebe had been less certain that it was a flattering term. She knew that Gregory's conciliatory tendencies disguised his fear of confrontation. He was easily intimidated by strong emotions in other people. He took a deep breath, entered the living room, and directed his attention to Sally.

'Hey, Sally.' His bonhomie struck such a false note that Sally moved to cover it.

'There are too many cars on the road, Gregory. I won't vote for you unless you ban them.'

Gregory managed a small laugh.

'I'm the minister for transport, not the minister for the abolition of transport.'

Her anger at Margaret's impertinence barely abated, Joyce said, 'I will do everything in my power, everything, to make sure that you don't get re-elected, Gregory. That is my solemn vow.'

'That's a bit heavy, Joyce,' Sally said. 'I was kidding.'

She was conscious of the fact that Joyce was resolutely refusing to make eye contact with her.

'Phoebe,' Joyce said, 'telephone for a taxi. I have to leave this house. I feel like the air I'm breathing is a contagion of moral corruption.'

'Has my deodorant failed me again? It's the lycra. It gets very sweaty and pongy.'

Phoebe smiled at Sally and moved to hug her. She wished Gregory had his sister's capacity for conjuring absurdity in awkward situations.

'You smell lovely, Sally, and stop being so dramatic, Mum.'

Joyce ignored Phoebe and turned again to Gregory. 'You're a whited sepulchre, Gregory, a whited sepulchre. I've said it before, but like all truths it bears repetition. You're all reason and conciliation on the surface, but it's a pose. A transparent pose.'

He found he couldn't let this go, not in front of witnesses.

'Why are you attacking me, Joyce? I respect the fact that you have strong opinions. I don't agree with them, but I respect your right to hold them and to express them.'

Joyce thundered.

'Opinions? Opinions? I do not have opinions! The word of God is the *word of God!* It is not an opinion!'

Margaret was disappointed to notice that Gregory actually blanched and made a small, involuntary shrinking movement away from Joyce.

There was silence in the room until Sally said, 'Still, it's not a fact, though, is it?'

Joyce, still staring at Gregory, her lip curled in contempt, said, 'Of course it's fact. It's more than fact. It's law, the law that controls all our lives, whether you know it or not and whether you like it or not.'

'Except where it's inconvenient,' Margaret said.

'Phoebe, will you please call that taxi?'

Phoebe raised her voice, an occurrence so rare that it took everyone by surprise.

'No, I will not! Gregory and I have news. Good news, and we're going to share it with you before you go storming out. This was supposed to be a lovely occasion.'

'Waving Gregory's private parts in my face wasn't likely to result in anything lovely, was it?'

Sally raised her hands in exaggerated puzzlement.

'I feel like I've missed something.'

'Gregory,' Margaret said, 'has had his portrait painted.'

'Vile! Vile! Vile!' Joyce said.

'Strong reaction, Joyce,' Sally said. 'It sounds promising. Who painted it?'

'Sophie White,' Gregory said.

'Oh, how exciting. She's very cutting edge. It's a coup getting painted by her. Good for you, Gregory.'

'It's in the dining room,' Margaret said.

Sally walked into the dining room, out of the sight of the others. They waited for her response. Each of them was looking in the direction of the dining room, rather than at each other.

'You see,' Sally called, 'this is why I'm a lesbian.'

Gregory sighed and joined his sister.

'Apart from the subject, do you like it?'

'Well I wouldn't say that I like it exactly. It's got your penis in it, so that's a bit of a deal-breaker right there. To be perfectly honest, my gut reaction is revulsion, but you know, that's a powerful emotion and I'm going to go with it.'

Phoebe, joining them, said, 'Revulsion is a bit strong, Sally. I think the painting is ghastly, but I'm not revolted by it.'

Sally didn't respond to this directly, not because she was offended but because she'd just noticed the expression on the portrait's face.

'Did you mean to be painted that way?'

'What way? Naked? Yes, of course. You don't end up accidentally being painted in the nude.'

'No, your face. You look slightly rapacious. Leering almost.'

'I look confident. Assertive.'

'Aggressive maybe.'

'Assertiveness and aggressiveness are not the same thing.'

Margaret, who was leaning in the doorway, said, 'Assertiveness is just aggressiveness with its hair combed and its tie straightened.'

As if to demonstrate the assertiveness and confidence that he saw in his portrait, Gregory aimed for firmness but landed on petulant defiance: 'I'm putting it in the Archibald. What do you think of that, Sally?'

'I think it's a great idea. The man behind the suit. That's what you should call it. Or maybe, *What Lies Beneath*.'

'It's *not* going in the Archibald,' Phoebe said. 'Don't encourage him, Sally.'

'I'm sorry,' Gregory said. 'The argument over whether or not it's going in the Archibald is over. While I was upstairs talking to Sophie, I sent her the signed permission electronically. I'm fully committed now, so there's no point arguing about it.'

As if to underline his resolution, Gregory walked back into the living room, where Joyce was still standing, waiting for someone to call her a taxi. The others ran their eyes over the portrait one more time, and each shook her head before returning to the living room.

'Abomination,' Joyce said. It wasn't clear whether this was directed at an individual or at the painting. Sally, who hadn't been privy to the earlier contretemps, assumed it was an opinion of the painting.

'It's bracingly unpleasant, Joyce, but that's because it's a picture of a naked man.'

'It's not just any naked man, though, is it?' Margaret said. 'It's the minister for transport, and it's my son.'

'It's still just a body.'

Every liberal fibre in Phoebe's being wanted to agree, but she just couldn't manage it.

'Would you be painted like that, Sally?'

'I would for Sophie White. In a flash. Although I'd try to look more approachable, and I'd do something about my bikini line.'

Joyce, who had no desire to turn her anger on Sally, said calmly, 'It's immodest, and flaunting the body is an abomination.'

Margaret couldn't help herself. She hadn't yet felt that she'd got the better of Joyce.

'You don't mind it when Jesus is writhing about in the nuddy on the cross, do you?' she said sourly.

'I do mind it, as it happens. Don't confuse me with the Catholics, Margaret. Christian doctrine needs to be taught in their schools too.'

'I think you'll find that Catholicism is a branch of Christianity,' Gregory said.

Joyce's view of Gregory could fall no lower without burrowing, and she dismissed what he said with a sharp, 'Hah!' The one thing she had in common with Margaret was an inability not to give in to the temptation to elaborate. 'Have you seen the Sistine ceiling?' She waved her hand. 'Of course you have. It was a rhetorical question. It's an obscene display of flesh masquerading as something sacred. It ought to be painted over.'

For Sally, who'd never thought Joyce's religiosity was anything more than a personal peculiarity, this was a truly astonishing and alarming thing to hear. The Sistine ceiling wasn't her favourite work of art. Every figure on it, including the female ones, was essentially male. Nevertheless, the idea that works of art might be attacked and obliterated was abhorrent to her. It smacked of Puritanism and Islamic State iconoclasm.

'You would paint over one of the greatest expressions of western art?' she said in horrified wonder.

'God is not impressed by pigment and perspective, and the man who painted it was a homosexual and homosexuality is an abomination.'

If Joyce hadn't been quite so wound up, she wouldn't have said such a thing in front of Sally. Too late, she saw the look of triumph that crossed Margaret's face.

'I'm sorry, Sally,' she said. 'I didn't mean to offend you. It's not for me to judge. I'm sure God loves you. It's only your homosexuality he loathes and finds disgusting.'

As a mollifying statement, this fell wide of the mark. Margaret said, 'God has nothing to say about lesbians, Joyce. He's not keen on gay men, I grant you, and recommends a good stoning in Leviticus, but he doesn't mention lesbians at all.'

'An abhorrence of one implies an abhorrence of the other.'

'No it doesn't!' Margaret's voice was beginning to assume a shrillness with which both Gregory and Sally were well acquainted.

'What it implies is that the men, the *men*, who wrote that stuff had so little respect for, or knowledge of, the sex lives of women that they couldn't even *imagine* the possibility of lesbianism.'

'God loves us all equally unless you betray that love with sinfulness.'

'He doesn't love dwarves equally, or blokes who've had their balls blown off by landmines, or eaten away by cancer.'

'Mum!' Gregory almost shouted. 'What are you talking about? What an absurd thing to say.'

'You weren't here for that discussion, Gregory, so never mind. I think perhaps you should tell your mother the news, Phoebe, before I kill her, an act that any sensible person would consider euthanasia.'

'Now we have your measure,' Joyce said. 'Drunk and violent.'

'Potentially drunk and potentially violent.'

'I feel only pity for you that a simple expression of Christian faith should provoke such unthinking rage.'

'It's really only creationism that gets my dander up,' Margaret said, half-humorously.

'I haven't even mentioned creationism.'

Gregory coughed, almost apologetically. 'Ah, you did mention it, Joyce. It's in your submission. I'm just reminding you for accuracy's sake.'

Margaret gave her son a small, appreciative nod and said, 'So is creationism a science or a spiritual belief,

Joyce? If it's related to faith, what place does it have in the science curriculum? If it's a science, what arguments and evidence can you marshal in its defence?'

'Evolution is just a theory. Creationism and intelligent design should sit beside it as legitimate, competing theories.'

'You don't understand the scientific meaning of the word "theory". Evolution is supported by rigorous scientific method, testing and proof. Creationism is a belief supported by ignorance and by people with a mental illness, low IQs, and learning difficulties.'

Joyce's face again started to flush as her anger rose.

'God cannot be reduced by science. He cannot be tested. It's a small mind that thinks that God can be contained in a test tube.'

In Sally's circle of friends and acquaintances, there were no Joyce Milfords. People like her existed as laughable-but-disturbing callers to talkback radio. They existed as a theoretical rather than an actual threat to the world she lived in. She'd been willing to accept Joyce as an aberrant and interesting visitor from another planet, someone who could provide her with an amusing anecdote about her brush with fundamentalism. This had shifted in the last few minutes into a determination to treat her with the disdain she'd richly earned by calling Sally an abomination and meaning it.

'There are more species of beetle on Earth,' she said, 'than any other, so if God is anything it's probably a beetle.'

Phoebe had been trying to quiet the rising agitation she'd been experiencing, and now she stepped forward to put an end to the discussions.

'I'd like everyone to sit down. Please. Mum, if you still want a taxi after you've heard our news, I'll call one for you. We'd prefer it if you'd stay to celebrate with us, of course.'

'Celebrate?'

Joyce made it clear in her enunciation of that single word that no celebration was possible in this house of sin.

'It's got nothing to do with my portrait, Joyce, so you can just put that out of your mind.'

'I can't *unsee* it. It will haunt me. I may wake up screaming.'

'If it goes on public display,' Margaret said, 'you won't be the only one. There'll be a big spike in night terrors across the country.'

'Please, please, please,' Phoebe said. 'Can we all calm down?' She began waving her arms about as if she were clearing the air of a bad smell. 'There's too much bad energy.'

'That'll be Sally's lycra,' Margaret said. 'It's creating enough static energy to feed into the grid.'

Sally, anxious now to support Phoebe, ignored her mother's put-down.

'All right,' Phoebe said, 'are all our tempers under control?'

'I have certainty, Phoebe, not anger.'

Phoebe could see that Margaret was about to respond to Joyce's comment and she put her hand out in the 'stop' signal.

'No!' She'd never spoken to Margaret so sharply before and Margaret felt it like a slap, which created a small chip in her previously well-varnished opinion of her daughter-in-law.

'Please, Margaret. Gregory and I would appreciate just a few moments of silence.'

Silence ensued.

'Thank you.'

It was broken as Sally's cycling shoes clattered noisily across the floor as she made her way to a chair. The clattering was briefly muffled as she crossed the thick carpet — an expensive and beautiful gabbeh — and started again on the other side. It put everyone's nerves on edge. Phoebe checked each of their faces to assure herself that no one was about to speak.

'Right. The reason that Gregory and I have asked you all here is nothing to do with his portrait. That was an unfortunate coincidence. Gregory and I  —' The doorbell rang. Phoebe threw her arms up in frustration.

'All right. I give in. I surrender. I'm pregnant. Gregory, please answer the door.'

Sally was about to respond, but Joyce beat her to it.

'Well that certainly settles the matter, doesn't it? That thing in there will have to come down. You can't raise a child with that in the house. Child Protection Services would need to be notified.'

'Seriously? Is that all you've got to say, Mum?'

'No, of course not. It's wonderful news. That hardly needs to be said, but there are priorities to consider, and the moral safety of your child is top of the list.'

Sally, who at this moment would have applauded if Joyce caught fire, hugged Phoebe and gushed in compensation for Joyce's chilly response.

'Oh, it's marvellous, Phoebe. Someone's coming into the world who's going to call me Aunt Sally.'

'Thanks, Sally. I appreciate your enthusiasm.'

Joyce made a small noise to indicate that she was aware of the slight, but that it was wasted. As far as she was concerned, she'd offered support and advice, and what more could be expected of her.

'I wouldn't mind having a child at some stage, and I'd like to be the one to carry it. I'd like to be in a relationship, though. Not that a child needs two parents necessarily.'

'You'll marry, of course,' Joyce said. 'Marriage will sort you out.'

'I'd love to marry. I just haven't met the right woman yet.'

Joyce was unable to hear this and maintain any pretence that Sally's sexuality wasn't abhorrent to her.

'The idea is grotesque and is an offence against everything that is decent.'

'My mother raised me to be polite, which is fortunate for you because if she hadn't I'd slap you so hard that your head would permanently face the rear.'

Joyce's face showed no dismay at this. Sally's words were entirely consistent with having been raised by Margaret, which wasn't too far from having been raised by wolves.

Gregory had caught the gist of all this as he went to the door. He was hoping it was just a delivery, something he could deal with quickly. When he opened the door, the last person he expected to see standing there, was standing there. This was the first time the state premier had called on him at home.

Louisa Wetherly was dressed in her uniform of a Chanel jacket and skirt. She had this outfit in a variety of colours, including pink, which always reminded Gregory of Jackie Kennedy clambering over the boot of that car to retrieve a piece of JFK's skull. Today she was in pale blue, with large sunglasses and sporting a new, severe haircut. Gregory recognised the homage to Anna Wintour. Louisa would have been surprised that he did so, but it wouldn't have improved her opinion of him. She was suspicious of men who knew things only women were expected to know.

Louisa liked Gregory, but only up to a point. He was young, not callow, but youthful — if a man in his early thirties could still be characterised as youthful. Youth wasn't an advantage in parliament. It was the enemy of gravitas, and Gregory had recently been saddled by a gossip magazine declaring him one of the sexiest men in politics, although the competition could hardly be called fierce. He'd done quite well as minister for transport, although he hadn't been tested. The state was going through an unusual period of union inactivity. There was, however, an election in the offing, so tensions were bound to arise.

'I hope I haven't come at an inappropriate time,' she said. 'I ought to have phoned ahead.'

Aware that the air in the living room was crackling with bad feeling, Gregory had no choice but to smile broadly, as if Louisa Wetherly's visit were a consummation devoutly to be wished, and to invite her in.

Louisa disliked the colour of the entrance-hall walls. She thought yellow made everyone near it look as if they had hepatitis. She didn't, of course, say anything. She tucked it away as a point against Gregory. In politics as in life it did no harm to maintain an archive of other people's weaknesses, including aesthetic ones.

Conversation in the living room had stopped just before Louisa and Gregory entered it. Gregory hurried to introduce her. He did it badly and sounded pompous.

'I'm sure you all know that this is our premier, Louisa Wetherly. This is my wife, Phoebe — you've met already, I think. My mother, Margaret; my sister, Sally; and my mother-in-law, Joyce Milford.'

There was something so absurd in his formality that

Phoebe knew she'd have to talk to him about it later. As it was, it threw her off slightly and she echoed it.

'I don't know what to call you. Madam Premier?'

'Louisa is fine.'

Joyce's eyes opened wide.

'You're the premier?' she said, just to have this confirmed.

'Yes, I am. Now, and after the next election.'

'Oh,' Joyce said, half to herself. 'God has brought you here.'

'Well no, it was Archie. My driver. He does have a high opinion of himself, but not that high.'

With practised charm, Louisa spoke to Sally.

'Gregory's sister. How lovely to meet you. A cycling enthusiast?'

Sally, who admired Louisa Wetherly, and who found her quite attractive, babbled. 'Oh yes. Not a lycra fetishist. There is a bicycle involved.'

Louisa laughed and it gave Sally a small thrill to feel it was genuine, not merely polite. Perhaps there was even something flirtatious in it. Was Louisa Wetherly gay, Sally wondered? No, she was fairly sure there was a husband, and children, lurking in the background — not that that proved anything. Still, the existence of a family would put a brake on any move Sally might make. She was conservative in her sexual advances and couldn't bear the idea that she might have been, in any of her relationships, a home-wrecker. She'd been the victim several times of other people's lack of squeamishness on this point.

Louisa couldn't fail to detect a certain froideur in the air, and while it didn't really make her uncomfortable — she quite enjoyed seeing conflicts played out that didn't involve her — she was sufficiently polite to apologise for the intrusion.

'I do seem to have disrupted a family occasion. I am sorry. I'll only stay for a moment. I just called in to …'

'Your minister for transport has exposed himself to me. To us all.'

It takes a moment to extract meaning from a statement like this. All the words are simple enough, but somehow they don't immediately make sense.

'Gregory exposed himself to you?' Even as she sought clarification, Louisa thought this was the strangest question she'd ever asked.

Joyce straightened her shoulders, ready to confirm what was for her an unarguable fact. She'd started the day with no interest in, or knowledge of, her son-in-law's penis. By midafternoon she felt she'd been slapped around the head with it. Phoebe quickly intervened.

'Not literally, Louisa. My mother is prone to unhelpful hyperbole.'

The puzzlement on Louisa's face required immediate relief.

'What my mother is referring to is a painting in the dining room.'

'Have you taken up painting, Gregory?'

'I've had my portrait painted. By Sophie White. I think it's bold and original, but opinion about its merits is divided.'

'I always think that's a sign of a good portrait,' Louisa said. 'Sophie White. I've heard the name, but I don't think I've seen any of her work. Is she any good?'

Just for a second, something passed across Gregory's face that might have been uncertainty. Phoebe noticed it. She was used to reading the slight movements among the muscles of his face. With a tiny note of triumph in her voice, she said, 'Aha! You're not as confident about it as you're pretending to be.' She hadn't meant to be quite so unguarded in front of Louisa Wetherly. If she'd been her own client, she'd have advised herself to keep her powder dry, and to not expose any disagreements in her marriage.

Louisa's interest in the portrait was now well and truly piqued, even more so when Gregory said, 'My view about the picture hasn't changed one iota. Is Sophie White any good? She's more than merely good. She's possibly great. I have to warn you though, Louisa, that you might find the painting challenging, but I also have to warn you that it will be put up for selection in this year's Archibald Prize. That decision's been made, and I've signed off on it.'

'I am intrigued. Why would a portrait of you be controversial? It's not as if you'd have been silly enough to get your gear off. Take me to it.'

Rather than point out that the assumption she'd made had been incorrect, Gregory led Louisa into the dining room. Margaret, Sally, and Phoebe followed. Joyce remained in the living room, where she conjured the more grotesque of the tortured figures in Bosch's version of hell. This calmed her down.

Louisa stood before the portrait. Her initial response was a simple, 'I see.'

'We're calling it *The Man Behind the Suit*,' Sally said.

Without taking her eyes off the canvas, Louisa said, 'Well there's certainly no sign of a suit. Goodness. I don't know what to say. I'm speechless. I am without speech.'

Phoebe was looking at Gregory, trying to see how he was responding to Louisa's eyes raking over his naked body. She thought she detected some discomfort. He wasn't naturally an exhibitionist. He was comfortable with his body, and he wasn't physically modest particularly, but he never wandered about the house naked. Despite his bravado, being stared at by strangers couldn't possibly be entirely pleasant.

'It's a good likeness,' Louisa said. 'I can only speak for the face of course. I'm assuming everything else is accurate. Is it?'

'Forensically,' Phoebe said. 'If you lean in, you can see a small freckle, right there, on the scrotum.'

Sally recoiled.

'That,' she said, 'is the ugliest word in the English language.'

'I never noticed it,' Phoebe said, 'until I saw it in the portrait. She must have got very, very close.'

'Her eye is trained to see small imperfections and to represent them honestly. She didn't as it happens get up very close.' In an effort to take people's attention away from his private parts — not an easy task given that they were at eye level — Gregory moved in front of the picture and faced the four women ranged before it.

'Forget that it's me, Louisa. Forget that it's someone you know. Imagine you'd come upon it in a gallery. What do you think of it as a work of art?'

Louisa hadn't risen to be premier by being vague about her responses to things. She was a pragmatic person.

'I can't forget that it's you, Gregory. It's obviously, ostentatiously you. Its value as a work of art comes a distant second to that simple, inarguable fact. It's you, and you're nude.'

'You have a female nude on the wall in your office. You're not going to tell me you disapprove of the nude in art.'

'It's a Picasso, and most people think it's a cucumber. I don't disapprove of the nude in art, or generally in fact. The nude in politics is new to me, and I'm not sure it will catch on.'

'This is art, Louisa. It's not a stunt.'

All four women were now looking at the flesh-and-blood Gregory Buchanan, who folded his arms defensively. It made him strangely uncomfortable, although he'd never admit it, to know that three of them were newly privy to what lay beneath his clothes.

Phoebe reached out and put her hand on Louisa Wetherly's shoulder, an oddly intimate gesture.

'Gut reaction, Louisa — Archibald or no Archibald?'

Without the slightest hesitation Louisa shot back, 'Oh there's no question about that. It can't hang in the Archibald, and Gregory knows that perfectly well. It would be political suicide. Scorn and ridicule would be heaped upon it from every quarter. Questions would be asked about it in the House. No, no, no, no, no.'

Gregory unfolded his arms and put his hands on his hips.

'Unbelievable. You're all philistines. You can't see the wood for the trees.'

'Unfortunate choice of words, darling,' Margaret said. 'You know, David went off and killed 200 Philistines and brought their foreskins back as a gift for his future father-in-law. I wonder if Joyce has a view on that?'

Gregory sighed.

'All you're seeing is the naked body. Try to see the *painting*.'

'Oh,' Phoebe said, 'we can see the painting. The painting is hard to miss. What's also hard to miss and what *you* can't see is that Sophie White thinks you're a dickhead. She's deliberately made your groin the focal point, and you can't seriously be flattered by the way she's painted your face.'

'A flattering portrait isn't a real portrait. I think we've had enough discussion.'

'No, Gregory. I'm serious. It was puzzling me why I really disliked it. I thought at first it was just the expression she's put on your face, but now I think the whole portrait is a joke at your expense. It's an elaborate one-liner.'

'I know you're trying to undermine my confidence, but it won't work, and as I said, I've signed the release for its entry in the Archibald, so I can't back out now.'

Gregory, with an unsightly show of exasperation, left the dining room and returned to the living room.

Louisa followed. She could see that her reaction to Gregory's portrait had disappointed him, or more correctly, irritated him. She'd been right not to applaud his decision, though. She didn't think it was courageous, or daring. She thought it was naive, or worse, foolish. She was confident though that the news she was about to give him would cause him to change his mind about putting his picture on public display.

'I can see how very determined you are to put that' — she waved in the general direction of the painting — 'in the Archibald, but I think you'll agree to keep it out of sight when I tell you why I've intruded so rudely.'

Joyce suddenly remarked, 'I have a petition. Gregory, where did you put my petition?'

The question seemed to summon the remaining women from the dining room. Phoebe said, 'This isn't the appropriate time, Mum.'

'The premier of the state is right here. What could be more appropriate?'

'There are proper channels, Joyce,' Gregory said. 'You can't just …'

Louisa, conscious that every vote would count in the next election, interrupted him.

'What's in your petition, Joyce? It's all right, Gregory, I'm happy to take it.'

'I don't think you will be, Louisa.'

A small, nasty part of Gregory was looking forward to seeing Louisa deal with Joyce's outrageous demands. It promised to be a satisfying revenge for her disapproval of his portrait. Trying not to sound too smug, he said, 'Joyce has a few changes she'd like to see implemented in the school curriculum.'

'Well I'm happy to listen. I can't just come barging in on a family occasion and offer nothing in return. My government is absolutely committed to improving educational opportunities. Any and all suggestions are welcome. Consultation is our mantra. It's the *mot juste*, the *raison d'être*, the *sine qua non* …'

With deep satisfaction now, Gregory said, 'Joyce feels that creationism ought to be taught in the science curriculum, to help balance the apostasy of evolution.'

This was too much for Joyce.

'I don't *feel* that it should. I *know* that it *must*. The word of God is not a *feeling*. It's not a *mood*.'

The outrage in her voice wasn't artifice. It was deeply, deeply felt.

'I see,' said Louisa, although she didn't see at all. 'How very interesting. I'll pass your petition on directly to the education minister. I'm sure he'll be delighted to deal with it.'

Joyce wasn't satisfied.

'I will not be fobbed off.'

'I'm sorry if I gave that impression, Joyce. I assure you, your views will be given the respect they deserve. I cannot, of course, promise you that your petition will succeed. The issue that you're raising is, as I'm sure you're aware, a contentious one. Gregory, where is the petition?'

Gregory looked around him, saw it on the arm of a chair, and handed it to Louisa. She looked at the cover page.

'Thank you, Gregory. Now, before we go any further, I must explain why I've called on you at your home. There's been an unexpected resignation from cabinet. The reasons are personal, but let's just say there may be a press conference where the minister's wife stands reluctantly at his side claiming that she trusts her husband and that the accusations against him are scurrilous. Needless to say, this is a disaster for us.'

After a brief pause, she said, 'This is yet another example of a bloke who couldn't keep his cock in his pants.' She hurried on before anyone could comment. 'I'm here to offer you the vacant position, Gregory. I say *offer*, but I'm actually insisting that you accept this promotion and the portfolio that goes with it. It's a big career boost for you, and a central plank in our re-election strategy. Joyce, I told you that I'd deliver your petition to the education minister.' With a great flourish, she handed the petition back to Gregory. 'Gregory, as the new education minister, may I present you with a petition from a valued constituent.'

The silence was broken when Joyce said, 'The good Lord moves in mysterious ways, his wonders to perform.'

As if at her invitation the hand of God took hold of Gregory's portrait and dashed it to the floor with a thunderous crash. This was how Joyce remembered it afterwards.

It took a moment for the shock of the sound to subside and for people to realise what had happened. Gregory dropped the petition on the floor and rushed into the dining room, where a little puff of plaster dust still hung in the air. The painting had fallen straight down to the floor, and then pitched forward. The appalling noise had been produced by the heavy frame slapping onto the expensive Italian tiles. Joyce, who'd taken a private oath to never set foot in the dining room while the horror remained on view there, now moved with the majesty of the vindicated to see the wreckage. The others followed.

'I think it's fine,' Gregory said. 'I don't think the painting has been damaged.'

'The wall on the other hand …' Phoebe said.

Joyce was smiling.

'The house itself rejects the abomination. It has vomited it forth.'

Gregory put his hands on his hips and looked directly at Joyce.

'The painting was too heavy for the load-bearing capacity of the picture hook. This is physics, Joyce, not divine intervention.'

'That is a distinction without a difference,' Joyce said.

'Sally, would you help me get this upright?'

Together, Gregory and Sally raised the picture and leaned it against the wall. Before its surface came into view, Joyce retreated to the living room. With some nervousness, Gregory examined the painting, and to his relief, and Phoebe's disappointment, there seemed to be no physical damage. There was a small scratch on one part of the frame. It had been Sophie White's decision to put the painting in a frame, despite its large size and the consequential expense. Gregory had thought her insistence on a frame was oddly conservative, but he was glad now that he'd accepted it.

Leaning at a slight angle against the wall, the picture's focal point was more obvious than ever. Louisa looked at Gregory and said simply, 'No.'

In the car on her way back to her office, Louisa asked Archie, her driver, if he'd ever thought about being painted in the nude. Archie looked in the rear-view mirror, half-expecting to find Louisa looking at him lewdly. He'd suspected for some time that she was attracted to him. He fancied that he'd caught her eyeing him off appreciatively on more than one occasion. There was that time, for example, when he'd had to change his shirt in the underground carpark after an accident with a hamburger. He always kept a spare shirt in the boot. He'd been summoned unexpectedly and had dripped tomato sauce down his front. Louisa had been in a hurry and had taken up her position in the back seat before he'd had a chance to change. He'd tried to be discreet by removing his shirt at the rear of the car, but his honed torso had filled the wing mirror and he'd realised that Louisa had been watching him. At any rate, he'd assumed this. The mirror was definitely in her sight line. She was way too old for him, of course, but he liked to think that the premier had the hots for him.

Having expected to find Louisa's gaze on him, he was a little deflated to find her distractedly looking down at her phone.

'I'm not sure I understand the question, ma'am.'

'If an artist, say a famous artist, asked you to pose nude for her …'

'Her?'

'Yes, her. If she asked you to pose for her in the nude, would you do it?'

'Is she good-looking, this artist?'

This question reminded Louisa that the difference between Archie's brain and a plank of wood was essentially an issue for forensics.

'The artist will charge you money to do the painting. Interested?'

Archie snorted and scratched the itchy patch on his chest, the legacy of a recent home waxing.

'Nah. If I'm going to get my kit off, I'm gonna get paid, not the other way round.'

Louisa lost interest in any further conversation with Archie. She began scrolling through her emails, and when Archie cleared his throat in what was an attempt to keep the conversation going, she ignored him.

He'd started to enjoy the images that popped into his head of himself being painted, and he assumed, wrongly, very wrongly, that Louisa must be enjoying similarly stimulating mental pictures. As he drove, the smile on his face spread, its increase matched to the increasing lewdness of his fantastical portrait session. By the time he'd parked the car in the parliament car park, the painting, a clichéd conglomeration of airbrushed, face-tuned blandness, had been abandoned by the female artist in favour of wrapping herself around his pliant, magnificent body. He needed to make a quick adjustment to his crotch before he got out of the car to open Louisa's door.

He wondered if she'd noticed that his pant front wasn't quite as flat as it ought to be. Louisa hadn't noticed.

Louisa Wetherly loved being the state premier. It wasn't about the power. Well it wasn't just about the power. It was undeniable that it was deeply satisfying to issue an instruction and have people scramble to carry it out. In her private life, such instructions went unnoticed or ignored by her two adolescent children. They were twins, a boy and a girl, now aged sixteen, and they were enjoying a carefully curated ennui. They were bored with their parents and bored with each other.

Louisa could understand their being sick to death of their father. She'd exhausted her interest in him within a couple of years of marriage. He left not long after the birth of the twins. He hadn't abandoned them. He'd always been a good provider, and Louisa had put up no roadblocks to his departure. They hadn't even really argued. There'd been no big blow up, no crockery thrown, no bitter words exchanged. On the contrary, in the final months of their marriage, few words were even spoken. Until the day Thomas left, they continued to share the same bed. They no longer touched each other, and the queen-sized mattress might as well have been a whole continent with each of them at either end of it.

Somehow, the afternoon Thomas packed his bags felt like any other afternoon. Louisa helped him carry his suitcases to the car, and he said, 'Right. That's it, then.'

Just for something to say, Louisa said, 'Where are you staying?'

'With a mate, until I get my own place.'

'You have mates?'

'We work together. You've met him. He's a beetle man.'

Thomas was an entomologist. He specialised in the larval stage of various insects. Louisa thought it was typical of Thomas to be drawn to the unformed version of a living thing. Once, he'd brought home a box of writhing white maggots, thinking she might find his work interesting. She'd looked in the box and then up into Thomas's expectant face, and her love, always feeble even at its strongest, had died.

Thomas wasn't a negligent father. He saw Josh and Juno every weekend and was always available to babysit. Louisa came to think of him as staff.

The premier's office was her demesne, and she thought the same about the floor of the House. She would much rather engage the leader of the opposition in fierce argument than attempt to do battle with her own children. She usually won in parliament; she never experienced victory at home. Juno especially could reduce Louisa to incoherent fury with just a sullen curl of her lip, and as soon as Josh had discovered that his mother hated tattoos, he'd begun tormenting her with the threat that he intended to get a facial tattoo the minute he turned eighteen. He decorated his walls with pages from tattoo magazines. Louisa was unable to disguise her disgust, which elicited from Josh his patented and infuriating smirk. Louisa loved her children; she was looking forward to liking them when the bullshit years were behind them.

Louisa's desk was the desk behind which all premiers sat. It was made from the timbers of a ship that had been wrecked off the southern coast of Victoria in 1854. There was nothing particularly significant about the wreck. It hadn't been carrying anyone of importance — no one of importance to the officials of the government of New South Wales, anyway. The family and friends of those who died — and all hands and passengers were lost — might beg to differ. Of course, by the time anyone back in England had been informed of the tragedy, the deceased had been that way for months. The most valuable thing about this ship had been its timbers, which washed up on a beach near Portland. Somehow, some of the wood had found its way to a master cabinet-maker, who worked for a full year to create a majestic desk, vast in size and weight, inlaid with expensive and rare woods, and finished with finely tooled leather and elaborate brass fittings. It had been purchased in 1890, at considerable expense, and had been ensconced in the premier's office ever since.

Louisa had disliked the desk at first. She hated the idea that the previous premier, whom she had ousted and whom she despised, had run his hands over it and dropped his dandruff on it. She went over it with disinfectant wipes, paying particular attention to underneath that part where her knees intruded. She dreaded to think what ghastly bodily detritus had been deposited there by an ear-waxed or mucousy finger.

Eventually, she came to love the desk. It was of a ludicrous size, and it wouldn't have escaped the accusation that it was florid even at the time of its creation. The IKEA generation would probably call it kitsch. Louisa too thought it slightly vulgar, but it was a defiant vulgarity.

As she sat behind it now, she thought of Gregory Buchanan, and her thoughts weren't positive ones. She'd been suspicious of him from the day he'd arrived in parliament. He was a career politician, there was no doubt about that, and the endgame for most career politicians was the leadership. Gregory Buchanan wouldn't consider that his career had been successful, no matter what portfolios he held, until he sat behind this gaudy desk. He'd proved himself to be a good performer, and he was popular in the party, so it would have invited comment if he wasn't rewarded with a cabinet position.

Yet Gregory's elevation to the education portfolio had been forced upon Louisa. He had a spotless reputation. He'd do a good job. She was confident of this. She was simply reluctant to promote him, because the higher he rose, the closer he came to unseating her.

Louisa closed her eyes for a minute and couldn't prevent an image of Gregory's portrait from floating up behind her eyelids. She tried to make it vanish, but it sat there stubbornly. When she opened her eyes, Anthony Acton was standing before her. He had a habit of doing this, of coming through doors without knocking on them first.

'Daydreaming?' he said.

Acton was Louisa's press secretary, although he liked to think of himself as being much more than that.

'The numbers aren't good,' he said. He liked delivering bad news. 'This is going to be one of the tightest elections on record. It's going to come down to mere handfuls of votes.'

'Whatever happened to safe seats?'

'Twitter. Facebook. People can barely make it to the end of a sentence. Thinking has become an archaic skill, like farriering.'

'As a press secretary, Anthony, I understand that your job is to lie …'

Acton raised a trimmed eyebrow.

'All right,' Louisa said, 'let's say "obfuscate". I'd like to think though that you don't … obfuscate with me.'

'The truth isn't always palatable. No one thanks you for telling the truth. However, I don't think I've ever been guilty of not being honest with you.'

He waited for a moment, expecting her to ask an exposing question. She didn't, mostly because Gregory Buchanan's genitals kept insinuating themselves into her mind's eye.

'You seem distracted.'

'I am distracted. I'll get to why in a minute. Tell me, of all the members of my cabinet, who do you like least?'

'Imelda Williams.' He delivered the name without the slightest hesitation.

'Oh?'

'She's not good at her job, she's lazy, she has a ghastly voice, which makes her a poor performer on radio and television, and when she wears high heels she walks like a wharfie.'

'Anyone else?'

'Matthew Adams.'

'I think he's doing a good job, or doesn't he know how to walk in heels either?'

'He isn't doing a good job. The public servants under him are doing a good job.'

'He performs well in parliament.'

'All his best lines are written by his wife. Once he's delivered them, he has nothing to say. Have you not noticed how bad he is at extemporising?'

'Is there anyone in cabinet you like?'

'No. The worst of them aspire to mediocrity; the best of them have achieved it.'

'What about Gregory Buchanan? It was partly your idea to promote him to education.'

'The competition wasn't fierce.'

'Do you like him?'

'He wants your job.'

Louisa leaned back in her chair.

'So do you, Anthony.'

Acton smiled.

'I don't want *your* job, Louisa. I may want *that* job, but if I'm ever in the position to put myself up for it, you will have long gone from this parliament. Gregory Buchanan, on the other hand, wants *your* job. He's ambitious. I'm not sure that he's sufficiently ruthless. Yet. He's still at that puppy-dog stage where he wants everyone to like him. Eventually he'll learn that he can't be the nice guy. Look like the innocent flower, but be the serpent under it. Isn't that the first rule of politics?'

'No, Anthony, that is *not* the first rule of politics, and I don't believe that you're that cynical.'

'Cynicism and realism are very much not the same thing. Why did you ask about Gregory Buchanan? There was a tone when you said his name. I'm very good at picking up tone. It's my superpower.'

'He's done something very silly, and he has plans to compound the silliness and create a disaster.'

Acton pulled up a chair and sat.

'Oh Christ, not another member of your cabinet who can't keep his dick in his pants.'

Louisa reached into the stupidly expensive Chanel clutch where she kept her phone.

'Gregory Buchanan has had his portrait done for the Archibald Prize. I surreptitiously took a picture of it, so it's a bit blurry, but I think you'll get the idea.'

She handed over her phone.

'Wait. This is a painting?'

'That's your first question? Not why the hell is the education minister stark naked?'

He stared a moment longer at Louisa's phone, then handed it back to her. A laugh escaped him.

'Funny?' Louisa asked. 'In case you haven't noticed, I'm not laughing. Not even a wry smile on this side of the desk, Anthony.'

'Isn't his wife in PR? She must be the shittest PR person in the state, possibly in the country, possibly in history.'

'It's not her fault. He didn't take advice before taking his clothes off for an artist who specialises in brutal photorealism.'

'You should delete that picture. I mean, clearly no one must see this painting. It can't go into the Archibald. I don't care if it was painted by Leonardo de fucking Vinci. Buchanan's career would be finished. He'd lose his seat. You'd lose the election. It's really very simple.'

'I have explained this to him, I assure you.'

'On the plus side, he'd never take your job. On the negative side, he wouldn't have to, because after the election you'd be leader of the opposition. At least until the next party-room meeting.'

Louisa drummed her fingers on the desktop. Acton had never seen her do this, and he assumed it meant she was experiencing an unusual level of stress.

'We can stop him, Louisa. I'll pay him a visit, and obfuscation won't figure in my discussion. If he won't listen to reason, I'll burn his house to the ground.'

Louisa narrowed her eyes at him.

'Oh my God,' he said. 'You actually believe I'd do that.'

Louisa picked up her phone and deleted the photograph of Gregory's portrait.

'I want to say no,' she said, 'but I have no real sense, even after working with you for this long, what the outer limits of what you're capable of are.'

Acton smiled broadly.

'Good,' he said.

Gregory's first day on the job as education minister was hectic. He wasn't the sort of politician who was content to let the people under him do all the work. At least initially, of course, the briefings were almost more than he could manage. He had meeting after meeting, and knew that he'd be reading late into the night for many nights to come. By 4.00 pm, he was exhausted.

He felt sweaty and wished he'd brought a change of shirt. He worried that the stress he was feeling was generating an offensive body odour, so he kept a window open even though it was cold outside. At 4.15, the person he least wanted to see, because he was the person he least liked, entered his chilly office without knocking. Anthony Acton stood before him and wrinkled his nose in distaste.

Gregory closed the folder he was holding and didn't give Acton the satisfaction of showing any irritation at his unheralded presence.

'Anthony.'

There was no rising terminal to suggest a question. It was simply uttering the name.

'Gregory.'

Gregory waited.

Acton waited.

Acton decided to cede some ground, mainly because he had a meeting with a journalist that he needed to keep. He had a minor leak to impart, and he was tempted as he looked at Buchanan to add the nugget that he'd seen the education minister's cock. It was way too early, though, to leak this. Buchanan would know that the information could only have come from Louisa. He'd hold fire on this one.

'I believe you're thinking of doing something so

epically fucking stupid that it should qualify you for a disability pension on the grounds that your IQ is so fucking low that the state is obliged to offer you a full-time carer to ensure that you don't leave the house with dags attached to your arsehole.'

It took Gregory a moment to unpick the elaborate invective.

'I won't pretend that I don't know what you're talking about. Clearly Louisa has spoken to you. However, I have no intention of discussing it with you. You're Louisa's press secretary, not mine.'

'Oh, there's nothing to discuss, Gregory. I didn't come here for a discussion. I just came here to gaze with wonder on the dumbest politician in the country. I've gazed, and now I'm finished gazing. I expect that your next job will be cleaning car windows at traffic lights.'

He shook his head in mock wonder, turned on his heel, and left.

Gregory was unimpressed. Anthony Acton could go fuck himself.

# Part
# TWO

As Phoebe pulled into the driveway of their house, she nudged Gregory awake. He'd been asleep for the past half-hour, which annoyed her a little. He'd been awake until they'd hit the outskirts of the city and had fallen asleep only when the traffic had become heavy. Phoebe felt like this was opting out. The least he could do was share the tedium of the crowded roads. He had, after all, until recently, been minister for transport. That test of mettle had been handed on to a junior woman.

Phoebe understood his fatigue. Of course she did. He'd been campaigning, they'd been campaigning, in rural districts for two solid weeks, living out of suitcases and wondering to each other how anyone could live in a town without a Gaggia.

At one point, Gregory had said, 'This is the longest two weeks of my life.' This was in response to a note pinned on the shower stall in an otherwise okay motel that read, 'Limit showers to three minutes. The hot water *will* run out. Do not shampoo. It will take 20 minutes to reheat the water.'

'I've only stayed in one other place where the hot water ran out,' he said, 'and that was in Laos.'

'The longest two weeks of your life? What about my life? I've taken leave to traipse around with you. If I never see another lamington, it will be too soon. And when did they start putting jam in them? What kind of person puts jam in a lamington?'

On the long drive home, Gregory had expressed his gratitude for Phoebe's support several times.

'You really didn't have to come,' he'd said, 'so I really appreciate that you did. It would have been a deadly two weeks without you.'

'Louisa wasn't very subtle in the pressure she applied. Apparently when the education minister does the rounds of country towns, the spouse is de rigueur. And a pregnant spouse is a real bonus. Country people like their politicians to be straight and fertile, like their livestock.'

Phoebe pressed the button to open the garage door, and Gregory stretched and yawned.

'God, it's good to be home,' he said.

'It's all over, darling, and you were terrific. You really were. I think people saw that you're decent and honest. I'm seriously thinking of voting for you. It is lovely to be back home.'

A door inside the garage led into the house. Gregory went to the keypad to disable the alarm. It had already been disabled.

'Phoebe! Did you set the alarm before we left?'

She came up behind him.

'That was your job. The alarm is always your job. Is there a problem?'

'The alarm isn't set. Now that you mention it, I do remember setting it. I'm sure I did.'

Phoebe cast her eyes nervously around the room. Nothing had been disturbed. There was no sense that a stranger had been inside the house.

'I must have just forgotten to set it. Sorry to give you a fright.' He kissed Phoebe lightly on the lips. She put her hand behind his head and held the kiss.

'Let's have a cup of tea before we unpack,' she said.

'I'll put the kettle on.'

Phoebe went into the living room, still feeling vaguely uneasy about the alarm. She touched a couple of objects, just to reassure herself that nothing had been interfered with. There was a diminutive Tanagra head of a woman, from the fourth century BC, which Gregory had given her on her last birthday, and which she treasured. She looked at it every day and wondered who'd owned it when it had been new. It was still in its place on the mantelpiece. Surely if someone had been in the house, this sculpture would have been taken. Its presence calmed her nerves, and she wandered into the dining room.

She didn't notice anything at first. In the days before they left for their regional campaign, Phoebe had become used to simply not looking at the portrait. Yet out of the corner of her eye, she sensed that something was awry. She turned to the picture and for a moment couldn't quite comprehend what she was seeing. The frame was intact, but the painting was gone.

'Gregory! Gregory!'

There was such panic in Phoebe's voice that Gregory rushed from the kitchen, thinking that she might be miscarrying.

'Are you all right? Are you all right? What's happened?'

Phoebe said nothing. She pointed towards the portrait. Gregory followed her finger.

'Oh my God! It's been cut out of the frame. We've been burgled!'

There was a stunned silence as they both stared at the empty space where the simulacrum of Gregory had once stood.

Phoebe whispered, 'What if they're still in the house? What if they're upstairs? They might have heard us come in and be hiding.'

'Should I check?'

Appalled by the question, Phoebe said, 'Of course you should check! Or do you want me to do it?'

'Yes, all right. I'll go upstairs.'

'You did judo, didn't you?'

'I was ten years old.'

'I'll call triple-O.'

'No! Don't do that. This isn't an emergency. It's just a burglary. Wait until I get shot.'

Phoebe suddenly realised that if there was someone upstairs, they might be dangerous or out of their minds on drugs and Gregory might indeed be in real danger if he went up there.

'Don't go upstairs! I'm sorry I snapped at you.'

Gregory held Phoebe and kissed her.

'I'm pretty sure there's no one upstairs. Why would there be? Ring the local police to report a burglary, and I'll just quickly check the house.'

Before Phoebe could protest, he headed upstairs. She waited a moment, half-expecting a shot to ring out. When nothing happened and Gregory called out that there was no one there, Phoebe took out her phone and called the local police. There was dial tone and it went immediately to a message.

'Your call is important to us. If your call is in relation to an assault, press one; aggravated assault, press two; assault with menaces, press three; assault with a deadly weapon, press four; assault with intent to cause grievous bodily harm, press five; assault with intent to kill, press six; murder, press seven. For all other inquiries, press eight. To hear these options again, press nine.'

Phoebe dutifully pressed eight.

'Thank you. Please hold. Your call has been placed in a queue. A police member will be with you as soon as one becomes available.'

Gregory returned just as the recorded message had run its course.

'What do the police say?'

'I'm in a queue.' She ended the call.

'This is ridiculous. I'm calling triple-O.'

'No. Do not do that. There's no one upstairs and no sign of any sort of disturbance. As far as I can tell, nothing has been taken. Your jewellery is still there, and our laptops. You can't ring emergency to report a stolen painting. They record the calls. It would be embarrassing.'

Phoebe could see the sense in this even though the thought that someone had been in their house felt violating and creepy.

The doorbell rang, making them both jump.

'Maybe that's the burglar,' Phoebe said, and she clutched Gregory's arm.

He didn't like the fact that her agitation was proving contagious, which is why there was a shortness in his tone when he said, 'No one's going to break into our house, steal something, and *then* ring the doorbell. It's probably Mum. She said she might drop in to hear about our trip.'

Phoebe thought that the person who chose to steal that frightful picture, and only that frightful picture, was fundamentally unwell and therefore capable of anything, including revisiting the scene of the crime and ringing the doorbell. She didn't express this, however, and Gregory went to answer the door. She remained where she was, mesmerised by the empty frame.

'It's all right, Phoebe,' Gregory called. 'It's just Sally.'

'What do you mean "just Sally"?' Sally said. 'Who were you expecting? The Pope?'

Gregory looked at his sister and just for a moment tried to imagine what the Pope would look like in the lurid lycra Sally was wearing.

'We've been burgled,' he said. 'Come in.'

'Oh no. How awful. They didn't crap in the bed, did they? Or piss in the fish tank? They do that apparently.'

'No, they didn't, and we don't own a fish tank.'

'Oh.'

'You sound almost disappointed.'

Sally was in fact disappointed, a little. She was conscious that there was a mean part of her that wanted what she saw as her brother's ordered, perfect life to be roughed up a bit. She loved him and she didn't envy him, but she just felt that over the course of their lives there'd been an uneven distribution of spanners being thrown into works. When they came into the living room, Phoebe joined them.

'What did they take? Secret cabinet papers?'

'They cut Gregory's portrait out of the frame and took that. Nothing else. Just that.'

Sally laughed.

'Why? Who would want … ? I mean, honestly, why would anyone … ?'

'Yes, all right, Sally,' Gregory said. 'We all agree, it's an unusual crime.'

'Have you reported it?'

'I can't get through to the bloody police, and Gregory doesn't want to call triple-O.'

'I'll call Carol,' Sally said. 'She's in my riding group. She's a police officer. I'm sure she'll come right over. She's very nice.'

Gregory immediately assumed an intimacy between Sally and Carol. His sister's sex life had always been more interesting and varied than his own.

'The local police should handle this,' he said.

'She can pass on the details, get the ball rolling. It'll be faster than waiting for the locals to turn up. She can give you good advice too.'

'Oh, all right. I hope she's discreet.'

'She's a police officer. Of course she's discreet.'

Phoebe looked worried. 'It's just that this is a singular sort of robbery, Sally.'

'It's just a picture,' Sally said, and moved away to ring Carol.

'This could be a disaster,' Phoebe said, 'a major public-relations disaster.'

'I wouldn't go that far,' Gregory said.

Phoebe had always been frustrated by Gregory's failure to appreciate the importance of PR. Apart from anything else, it meant that he didn't really understand her career. He would always listen attentively to her descriptions of her daily engagements, but he rarely offered advice. He was sympathetic when she was cross about some issue at her office, and yet there was a lingering sense that he wasn't entirely sure what it was all about. She was particularly irritated when he expressed the belief that PR was essentially 'spin'.

'You finally saw sense, darling, about putting your portrait in the Archibald Prize, so the only people who got to see it were visitors to this house, which means our respective families. Now someone has made off with it.'

'It wasn't a question of seeing sense. I stand by the integrity of that portrait. I happen to agree, though, that as minister for education it wasn't a good fit.'

'So there are nude-appropriate portfolios, are there?'

Gregory thought about that.

'Yes, I believe there are. Aged care perhaps.'

Phoebe laughed.

'At least you know how ludicrous that sounds. What if you'd become education minister *after* it had been hung in the Archibald?'

'Oh yes, all right. I concede the point, and I agree that we now have a problem. I won't go so far as to say that the portrait was a mistake, but I will admit that, for the moment, it should enjoy a limited audience, and that that audience shouldn't include the state's primary-school children.'

Sally returned and said that her friend Carol was on her way. 'I didn't give any details. I just said that there'd been a burglary, and she knows it's sensitive on account of who Gregory is.'

'I should phone Louisa,' Gregory said. 'She's coming over later for a debriefing on our tour.'

'No,' Phoebe said, with surprising sharpness. 'What if she organised to have it stolen?'

An involuntary laugh escaped Gregory.

'What? You think Louisa Wetherly organised for someone to break into our house and steal the picture? Why? That's a bit QAnon, isn't it?'

Slightly chastened by the QAnon reference, Phoebe said, 'There are only a few people who know the picture even exists.'

'So?'

'So we have to think about who might want it and why. It wasn't a random theft. It was targeted.'

'This isn't Cluedo. Let's leave that up to the police,' Gregory said.

Phoebe had begun to seriously ponder the implications of the theft.

'We're all suspects — even you, Gregory. Every one of us has a motive for keeping that portrait out of the public eye.'

Sally, who'd also begun to think about the crime — and frankly, to be entertained by it — said, 'Oh, what if the motive was to make sure it made its way into the public eye?'

'Oh my God!' Phoebe said. 'I hadn't thought of that.

Sophie White! She *was* furious when you withdrew permission to hang it in the Archibald.'

Sally had been reading crime fiction, and she asked urgently if there'd been any sign of forced entry.

'Did you check the alarms?' she asked.

The tone of Sally's enquiries was making Phoebe nervous.

'They were switched off.'

Sally nodded knowingly.

'Interesting,' she said. 'Very interesting.'

'No it isn't,' Gregory said firmly. 'I may simply have forgotten to set them. I can't recall whether I did or didn't. We were running late.'

The doorbell rang again and all of them jumped.

'I'm changing that doorbell,' Gregory said. 'I never realised how frightening it is. That will probably be Mum.'

When Gregory had left, Phoebe said, 'You didn't take the painting, did you, Sally?'

The look on Sally's face made her immediately regret the question. She added pathetically, 'It's just that you were very keen to see it in the Archibald.'

'Good God, Phoebe. What is wrong with you? What a grotesque suggestion!'

Phoebe back-pedalled.

'Yes. I'm sorry. I'm in a bit of a flap. I'm not thinking clearly.'

Sally wasn't quite ready to be mollified.

'I was definitely in favour of hanging it in the Archibald. I thought it was brave. However, of course I respect Gregory's decision not to go through with it. I was disappointed. I think it was a failure of nerve, and just once in his life I was hoping he wouldn't be guilty of that. Did you really think that I would steal it and show it to people without his permission?'

Phoebe was used to charming-Sally. Tough-Sally was a surprise.

'Anyway,' Sally said. 'You hated the picture. You didn't organise to have it removed while you were away, did you?'

Phoebe felt that an outraged response would have been hypocritical, so she tried to make her voice neutral.

'I did not. I can't honestly say that I'm heartbroken that I don't have to look at it, but I'm very, very concerned. I'd rather it was someone we knew who took it. I just hate the idea of my house being violated by a stranger, especially a stranger with sinister motives.'

Gregory returned accompanied by Margaret, whose jubilant expression suggested that she'd been told the news and that she considered it good news.

'I have mixed feelings,' she said. 'I'm both shocked and delighted.'

'There's no reason to be delighted, Mum. You know I'd decided not to exhibit the picture.'

'It's not hanging in the dining room, Gregory. That's a little bit delightful. Why aren't the police here? You have called them?'

'A friend of Sally's is on her way,' Phoebe said. 'She's a police person. Our local police don't offer stolen paintings on their menu of offences.'

Margaret had no idea what this meant but was too preoccupied with the news of the break-in to seek clarification.

'Joyce will be thrilled,' she said. 'She will have been praying for this. The fact that it's actually happened will form one of her proofs for the existence of God. Oh, I just had a wicked thought. You don't think Joyce took it, do you?'

Returning to his benign view of Joyce, Gregory expressed horror at his mother's suggestion.

'Honestly, Mum, sometimes you say the most ridiculous, and yes, offensive things.'

Margaret shrugged. Phoebe came to her defence.

'It's a perfectly reasonable supposition. My mother is capable of doing almost anything in the name of Jesus. She wants to paint over the Sistine ceiling. She wouldn't bat an eyelid at destroying that painting. Temporal laws and God's laws are two very different things for her.'

'But breaking and entering, Phoebe. Come on.'

'She has a key and nothing's been broken.'

'If it comes to that,' Sally said, 'we all have keys to the house and we all know the alarm combination.'

The truth of this observation struck them all. The doorbell rang, which made all four of them jump.

'Jesus,' Sally said, 'I've never noticed before what a

nerve-jangler that is. That will be Carol. She wasn't far away.'

Gregory went again to answer the door. In his brief absence, Sally said, 'I know it's terrible, Phoebe, but it's also exciting, don't you think? An actual art heist.'

'No, Sally, I don't think it's exciting. All sorts of horror scenarios are running through my mind. What if it ends up on eBay? What if the opposition gets hold of it?'

When Gregory led Carol into the room, all eyes turned to her. Like Sally, she was outfitted in tight lycra. Gregory was discomfited by the fact that an image of the Willendorf Venus had popped into his head. He couldn't discipline the vagaries of the male gaze into complete submission, although he'd learned never to comment on a woman's body in either a positive or a negative way — at least not in front of his wife. Occasionally, he was guilty of breaches of woke etiquette among male friends, and as a rider to these conversational breaches it was always declared, 'I can only say that here.'

Carol took off her cycling helmet and addressed the room.

'Senior Sergeant Carol Hinton. I came as quickly as I could. Where's the body?'

Sally stepped forward.

'Ah, I may have given you the wrong impression, Carol. Or rather, I may have given you a *heightened* impression. A body *is* involved, in a way, and I needed you here quickly.'

Carol didn't attempt to disguise her annoyance.

'This is my day off, Sally. I thought this was urgent.'

'Oh it's urgent. I wouldn't have called you here on a whim.'

The look Carol gave Sally was discouraging of Sally's hopes of a relationship. And the frankly appreciative looks Carol was giving Gregory offered further discouragement.

'May I just, Mr Buchanan … ?'

'Please, call me Gregory.'

'May I just say, Gregory, that it is a pleasure to meet you. I think you're doing an excellent job, and if you don't mind me saying so, you look very good on television. What is it you need me to do?'

This was such a peculiar follow-up to her remarks to Sally that Gregory simply didn't engage with them. Instead he said, 'This is my wife, Phoebe, and my mother, Margaret. Sally you already know.'

Carol slipped into as professional a mode as her attire would allow.

'Perhaps you could tell me what has happened here, Gregory.'

'We've been burgled. Well, we think we've been burgled.'

'In my experience, Gregory, if you don't mind me saying so, burglary isn't a particularly vague crime.'

Carol's open admiration of Phoebe's husband had not gone unnoticed by Phoebe. She wasn't in the least jealous. She'd just spent two weeks watching women, and some men, mooning over Gregory.

'What my husband means, Carol, is that though there doesn't seem to have been any forced entry, an extremely valuable painting has been stolen.'

Ignoring Phoebe, Carol focused all her attention on Gregory.

'I see. This painting, Gregory, could you describe it?'

She took a notebook from the bum bag that sat under her belly's overhang, and prepared to take notes.

'It's a portrait of me as a matter of fact. That's not what makes it valuable. It's by Sophie White, who is a well-known and well-respected artist.'

'And where was this painting stolen from?'

Gregory ushered Carol into the dining room. Phoebe, Margaret, and Sally followed. Gregory indicated the empty frame.

'It fell off the wall. It was too heavy for the hook.'

'It must have been a very large portrait, Gregory.'

'It was a full-length portrait, and slightly larger than life size.'

Carol's lips formed into a moue, as if despite her apparent approval of Gregory in the flesh, the idea of so ostentatious a display of him on canvas spoke of self-confidence that was off-putting and suspect.

'Well, it shouldn't be too hard to track down, if it was a good likeness.'

Margaret had been uncharacteristically quiet. She broke her silence.

'My son is withholding one fairly pertinent piece of information, Carol.'

'I wasn't withholding it. I was getting to it.'

When he didn't immediately get to it, Carol asked, 'And what might this pertinent piece of information be?'

Gregory sighed and put his hands on his hips.

'It's a nude portrait, Carol.'

Carol took a moment.

'You mean you're in the nuddy, Gregory?'

'That is generally the case with nude portraits, Carol.'

'I see. And it's full-length, you say.'

'And larger than life,' Sally offered.

Her pen poised, Carol said, 'I'll need a full description.'

'There's nothing to describe,' Gregory said.

'I'm sure that's not true, Gregory.'

Choosing not to acknowledge the inappropriate loucheness of Carol's tone, Gregory said, 'It's a portrait, Carol. It looks like me. I would have thought my face would do as a distinguishing mark.'

This wasn't enough for Carol.

'Are you standing or sitting?' She paused. 'Or reclining.'

Gregory looked at Sally in a manner that made it clear that he was blaming her for the presence of this prurient police officer.

'Don't think Titian's *Venus of Urbino*, think Sargent's *Lord Redesdale*.'

'I have no idea what that means,' Carol said. She was aware that Gregory was trying to put her in her place. Her admiration of him began to drain away.

'It means that I'm standing.'

'I don't mean to exasperate you, Gregory, really I don't, but we do need a proper, detailed description of the painting. Maybe you could show me how you were standing.'

'Is that really necessary?'

Carol smiled.

'It would be useful.'

Gregory struck a reluctant and embarrassed pose. He put one hand on his hip and let the other drop to his side. To preserve some sense of dignity, he said, 'An educated observer would see it as a reference to swagger portraits, which have a long and distinguished history.'

Margaret couldn't let this art-historical justification go unremarked upon.

'And he's wearing an expression that is more than usually smug,' she said. 'I'm sorry, darling, I *am* trying to be helpful.'

'I wouldn't call it just smug,' Phoebe said. 'I'd call it venal.'

'Smugly venal,' Sally said.

Carol was jotting everything down. Margaret cruelly thought that Carol would have to look up the meaning of 'venal' later. She was wrong about this. Senior Sergeant Carol Hinton was very good at her job and had quickly taken the measure of every person in the room. She would admit to herself afterwards that she'd been too easily impressed by Gregory Buchanan's appearance, but was equally pleased to acknowledge that she'd reassessed her opinion of him within a very short time.

Carol put away her notebook and said that she wanted to check all the entry points in the house. She didn't need a guide. She'd find her own way.

Phoebe had never thought of her house having entry points, and shuddered. Carol's presence wasn't making her feel secure. Quite the reverse.

'I don't have much confidence in your friend, Sally. She was making cow eyes at Gregory.'

'Was she?' Gregory said. 'I didn't notice.'

Sally had been disappointed in Carol's reaction to Gregory. It made her doubt the accuracy of her gaydar, but it didn't entirely extinguish her hopes.

'She's probably never had a case like this before,' she said. 'How often do you think she gets asked to locate stolen nude portraits of members of parliament?'

Phoebe instigated her default peace-making move.

'I'll make us all a cup of tea.'

Margaret's default position was to disrupt peace-making moves.

'You haven't set your bicycle helmet for this woman, have you, Sally?'

'What a revolting expression, Mum, but I'd be

lying if I said I'm not a little disappointed by Carol's behaviour. I did think …'

'Oh, darling, she's far too old for you.'

'She's only in her forties, Mum, and I prefer mature women.'

'When does maturity slide into gerontophilia?'

Gregory wondered if his mother's capacity to say dreadful things would ever weaken. Trying to support Sally, he said, 'Has she given you any encouragement?'

'I haven't broached the subject with her, and I think we might need to change the subject.'

Margaret wasn't ready for a subject change.

'You always want to change the subject when the subject is your relationships. I want to be supportive.'

'Thank you, but my sex life hasn't deteriorated to the point where it requires support.'

Margaret ploughed on.

'That isn't what I meant. I want to understand, to celebrate, to see things through your eyes. Carol, for instance. What on earth do you find attractive about her? She has the sexual magnetism of a dugong.'

This observation went unchallenged, not because Sally or Gregory agreed with it, but because neither of them could quite believe that she'd said it.

'I think,' Gregory said, 'that we have stumbled on the explanation for Sally's reluctance to discuss her private life with you, Mum.'

Phoebe's return with the tea things broke the

conversational thread. Gregory tried to keep it broken by beginning to talk about his tour of the regions.

'We did a really good event in …'

The name of the regional town was lost beneath Sally's 'Dugong? Dugong? Also, I believe, called a sea cow.'

Margaret wasn't prepared to admit that perhaps she'd gone too far, but as a kind of apology she offered, 'Well, you're assuming I meant that pejoratively. Early sailors thought dugongs were mermaids, and everyone loves a mermaid.'

Phoebe had missed the beginning of this conversation and wasn't anxious to have it explained to her. Sally's expression was enough to alert her to the undesirability of an expansive explanation. She poured the tea and said, 'We'll talk about the tour later. Right now, your stolen portrait is the only thing anyone is interested in, and I do think the prime suspect is my mother. I'm absolutely with Margaret on that. She thought that picture was a manifestation of the devil's work in the world, and she admitted to being in favour of destroying works of art that she considers offensive, and I know that you suspect her as much as I do, Gregory.'

Gregory began to object, but lost impetus.

'But to say it out loud, Phoebe. It just sounds so awful.'

'Should we say something to Carol?'

'You want to shop your mother to the cops?'

Phoebe shrugged.

'You do the crime, you do the time, Gregory. Isn't your government trying to look like it's tough on crime?'

Margaret's face was beaming.

'Oh yes,' she said, 'bring Joyce in for questioning.'

'I think this whole thing is bringing out the worst in all of us,' Gregory said.

Carol heard this last comment as she came back into the room.

'Any sort of trauma is a real test of character,' she said. 'Some people are at their best, and as you say, some people are at their worst.'

She gave no indication whether she saw evidence of either of these reactions here.

'There's no evidence of forced entry. All the windows are locked and haven't been tampered with, and the door locks show no sign of damage. I'd say that whoever took the painting entered the house using the key and knew how to disarm the alarm. Either that or we're dealing with a very skilled, professional burglar. If that's the case, this painting must be a very big deal, Gregory. Who has a key to this house?'

Gregory thought for a moment.

'Phoebe and I, of course, and Sally and Mum, and Phoebe's mother, Joyce.'

'What about a cleaner?'

'No, we don't employ a cleaner,' Phoebe said. 'I don't

like strangers poking around the house.'

Carol clattered across the room in her cycling shoes — they were briefly silenced by the rug — and sat down in an armchair. She produced her notebook.

'I just need a few things in order here to pass on to the official, investigating officers. Now, you and Phoebe have been away?'

'Yes,' Gregory said. 'For two weeks, in the country. I was campaigning. I did return for one night in the first week, and the painting was still here then, because I looked at it.'

'I see,' Carol said, and her tone suggested that there might have been something sinister about this visit home. 'Did your wife accompany you?'

'No. Phoebe had a CWA function.'

'That's right,' Phoebe said. 'I couldn't get out of it without offending people.'

'I see,' Carol said. 'Now, when you say that this picture of you in the nuddy was valuable, how valuable are we talking?'

Gregory had become secretly ashamed of the amount he'd paid to Sophie White.

'It's worth at least ten thousand dollars.'

'That's what you paid for it,' Phoebe said. 'It isn't necessarily what it's worth.'

'Hmmm,' Carol said. 'That sort of value puts it out of the hands of uniform. This is a CIB job. They'd appreciate a proper briefing, so if you don't mind I'd like to ask everyone a few questions. You're under no obligation to answer them, but it will be helpful and will save time further down the track.'

The doorbell rang and everyone jumped.

Phoebe went to answer it, having forgotten the possibility she'd raised that it might be the burglar returning to the scene of the crime.

'I can ask my questions in private,' Carol said. 'I don't want to be impertinent or offend anyone.'

Before anyone could answer, Phoebe came back into the room, accompanied by her mother, sensibly dressed as always in dun-coloured clothes. Also, as always, Joyce was on a mission, and after the briefest of glances around the room, and feeling no need to acknowledge anyone, she said simply, 'Gregory, I have a more comprehensive petition and ten, *ten*, more signatures.'

Speaking as if her mother had made no utterance at all, Phoebe said, 'This is my mother, Joyce Milford. Mum, this is Senior Sergeant Carol … ?'

'Hinton. Carol Hinton. Excellent. So all the key-holders are now here.'

'What is this woman talking about?' Joyce asked.

Margaret took the opportunity to speak.

'We're all suspects in a burglary and a theft, Joyce.'

'I beg your pardon? Are you inebriated already?'

'Sadly no. I'm going to have to listen to you sober.'

Another argument between his mother and Phoebe's

mother was too much for Gregory, and he moved to head it off.

'My portrait has been stolen, Joyce. Somebody came into the house while Phoebe and I were away and cut the painting out of the frame.'

Joyce held the rolled-up petition against her chest.

'Oh God is good and God is great, and he moves in mysterious ways, his wonders to perform.'

'Surely you're not condoning theft?' Margaret asked.

'I hate the sin but love the sinner.'

'You wouldn't be that sinner, would you Joyce?'

'Mum!' Gregory was genuinely appalled, and his face flushed blotchy red with anger. Carol could see that there was nothing to be gained from this bickering and again took control of the proceedings.

'A crime has been committed here, Joyce, and I was just about to ask individuals a few questions. As I told everyone here, this is not a formal interview, and you are not obliged to answer my questions. I'm not on duty, so this is all very informal. I'm just trying to help out before handing over to the CIB. Are you okay with answering a few questions? We can do it in private if you'd prefer.'

Joyce tapped the petition against her bosom.

'I have grave objections to being under some sort of suspicion. The very idea! As if I could bear to look at, let alone touch that vile object, that abomination. Just the thought of it makes me ill.'

Carol wasn't yet taking notes, but she was noting

every small nuance of people's posture and behaviour.

'It isn't quite a question of suspecting you of having committed a crime, Joyce. I'm sure you'll be relieved to be eliminated from our inquiries.'

Joyce snorted.

'Oh go ahead. Ask away. I don't require privacy. I have nothing to hide.'

Carol flipped open her notebook.

'I take it from your description of Gregory's portrait as an abomination that you thought its artistic merits were questionable.'

'I don't believe that a picture of my son-in-law naked has any merit of any kind — artistic, moral, social. *None of you shall approach to any that is near of kin to him to uncover their nakedness. I am the Lord.*'

'I see,' said Carol. 'That seems fairly unequivocal. Have you visited the house in the last fortnight?'

'Yes, I have.'

Gregory's and Phoebe's mouths fell open.

'Mum!'

'There's nothing sinister about it. I let myself in with my key with the intention of leaving my new petition in plain view. Then I thought better of it.'

'What day was this?' Carol asked.

'It was Thursday, in the first week of their absence.'

'And was the painting here then?'

'I have no idea. I didn't soil my sight by going into the dining room.'

'I *knew* I'd armed the security alarm,' Gregory said. 'Did you re-arm it when you left, Joyce?'

'Probably — or more accurately, possibly. It's such a fiddle.'

'That was irresponsible, Mum. You left our house vulnerable, and someone took advantage of it, and however you feel about Gregory's painting, it's *Gregory's*, no one else's.'

Joyce wasn't in the least chastened.

'Filth is owned by the devil.'

Phoebe knew there was no use arguing. 'I'll make us a fresh round of tea,' she said.

Joyce remained standing, which made everyone feel uncomfortable. She declined an offer to sit down, saying that she wasn't going to stay long. As soon as the petition had been safely delivered, she'd get Gregory to call a taxi and she'd be off.

'I would like to speak to it before I go, however. I can do that now.'

This didn't suit Carol. She wasn't intimidated by Joyce, despite Joyce's conscious and unconscious effort to impose her will on those around her. Joyce was a faint echo of Carol's sister, who was by any measure a religious fanatic. She'd begun by joining the Jehovah's Witnesses and had been happily 'disfellowshipped' by them. She'd found them weak and fatally hamstrung by their charisma-free male leadership. It was a boys' club, with surrendered wives — and all boys' clubs, according to Carol's sister, were essentially homosexual in nature. She'd gone rogue, aligning herself with no faith but modelling herself on ecstatic saints like Thérèse of Lisieux and Francesca Romana. She'd taken to falling into paralysed states of 'ecstasy', and like her heroine Veronica Giuliani, licking the floor in an act of holy self-abnegation. She was also prone to inexhaustible fits of rage where she would subject those around her to hours of lacerating condemnations of their sinfulness. Joyce by comparison was a paragon of restraint.

'I'm sorry, Joyce,' Carol said, 'I'd like to get my questions out of the way if that's all right.'

Although this wasn't all right, Joyce held fire. Sally put down her teacup and said, 'I'll go next, and I'm happy to answer questions in front of everyone. This is all very Poirot.'

Carol hadn't made up her mind about Sally. She was aware of Sally's attraction to her, and she was flattered by it because Sally Buchanan was an attractive woman. However, she didn't really like Sally's family. They would always do and say the *right* things. They were good people. Probably. However, it was untested goodness. They would sincerely declare how much they despised injustice, without ever having experienced it. She was suspicious of them, and some of this suspicion fell on Sally.

'I'll ask you the same question I asked Joyce. Have you been at the house in the last fortnight?'

'Categorically no.'

'Did you give your key and perhaps the alarm code to anyone else?'

'Carol! No. Why would I want to steal Gregory's portrait? He's naked, and he's a man, which is a deal-breaker for me, and he's my brother, so there's a whole incest thing there.'

'Abomination,' said Joyce.

'Well, that's the question, isn't it?' said Carol. 'Why would someone want to target this particular item? Any ideas? Anyone? I feel like there's an important piece of information that I'm missing.'

Phoebe returned with yet more tea things.

'The missing piece of information, Carol,' Phoebe said, 'is that Gregory initially had the ludicrous idea that he'd hang the portrait in the Archibald.'

Phoebe looked at Gregory, expecting him to interrupt. He didn't.

'All of us were horrified.'

'Just for the record,' Sally said, 'I was in favour of hanging it in the Archibald. I still am.'

'All of us, apart from Sally, were horrified. The premier was here the day the portrait arrived — just by coincidence — and she of course thought Gregory's idea was madness. We knew that it would kill his career and perhaps even cost the government the election.'

Margaret, eager to help, said, 'Gregory, despite knowing that this election is on a knife edge, dug his heels in, something he's done since he first learned to walk.'

Gregory believed that his stubbornness in childhood was a myth.

'I did not dig my heels in. I merely mounted a defence of the portrait as a significant work of art and therefore above the petty prejudices of the ill-informed, the insensitive, and the hysterical.'

Gregory had a way of lifting his chin slightly when he spoke like this, and a small part of Phoebe died every time he did so. Carol also found this mannerism off-putting, but didn't show it.

'So you think it might have been stolen to prevent you putting it on public display?'

'That would have been pointless. I'd already decided against hanging it, and besides, only a few people knew that the picture even existed. I never mentioned it to any of my colleagues. The premier knew, but she wouldn't have gossiped about it. As far as she was concerned, the fewer people who knew about it the better.'

'How did the artist take the news?' Carol asked.

'She was furious. I don't blame her. I'd given her a commitment, and now I wasn't going to honour it.'

'I see.'

'What do you see?'

'I see that there are people outside this room who have an interest in the fate of the painting.'

'Good God, you don't seriously think that either the

premier or Sophie White organised to take it. That's just too absurd. How would they manage a break-in?'

Carol narrowed her eyes.

'That's for the CIB to sort out. I'm just canvassing possibilities to provide a comprehensive brief. I'm not here to form an opinion or make a judgement.' She was beginning to enjoy herself. 'However, since you asked how an outsider might manage a break-in, the most obvious way is with the help of an insider.'

'One of us?' Sally said.

Carol smiled, aware that this little seed might sow suspicion and discord, and wasn't displeased by this. She wasn't entirely right about the sowing, given that both Margaret and Phoebe already harboured serious suspicions about Joyce, although neither of them believed that she might be in cahoots with either Sophie White or the premier. Sophie White especially was an unlikely ally for Joyce. Phoebe decided to take a sensible approach.

'Look, it's obviously one of us. The idea of a state-sponsored burglary is ridiculous. We could clear this all up if the person who took it stepped forward now.' She left a pause, of which no one took advantage. 'No one's going to press charges. We won't even quiz you about it. Perhaps it was a misguided attempt to protect Gregory from himself. If the painting is returned, we'll say no more about it. That's right, isn't it, Gregory?'

'Yes, yes, of course.'

'You're assuming,' Carol said, not willing to let go of the possibility of discord, 'that Gregory didn't remove the picture himself. Was it insured?'

'Of course it was,' Gregory said. 'It was insured for what I paid for it, ten thousand dollars.'

'So given that you'd decided against showing it, it was an expensive purchase to just have hanging on the dining-room wall. A suspicious detective might think that you could steal it, hide it, and get your money back on the insurance claim. And you'd still have the painting.'

What had happened to fawning Carol? Sally didn't much care for Rottweiler Carol, and she could feel anger directed at her from both her mother and her brother.

Phoebe, who hadn't actually considered the possibility of Gregory stealing his own portrait, wasn't going to give Carol the satisfaction of showing any dismay. Carol was baiting them, and Phoebe wasn't going to take the bait.

'I'm not assuming anything, Carol, and I agree with you that that is an entirely plausible scenario, or it would be if Gregory weren't Gregory.'

Margaret cleared her throat. She wasn't as convinced as Phoebe was that Gregory wasn't capable of enacting Carol's suggestion, but she felt a maternal duty to take some of the heat off him.

'This might be the moment,' she said, 'to admit that I let myself into the house while Phoebe and Gregory were away. I think it was Wednesday, the day before Joyce says she was here. I thought I'd left a brooch here on the afternoon Phoebe told us she was pregnant. I hadn't left it here, as it turned out, but I was anxious about it. It was one of my late husband's rare, tasteful choices of gift.'

'I see,' Carol said. 'And the painting?'

'Oh it was here. I glanced at it, just to assure myself that a naked portrait of my son isn't a positive contribution to the culture.'

'It's an abomination,' said Joyce, who was still standing rigidly in one spot. She was like a very dull version of Stanley Kubrick's monolith in *2001: A Space Odyssey*, Sally thought.

Carol had been diligently taking notes, and she added Joyce's 'abomination' for the second time.

'So,' she said, 'we know the painting must have been taken some time in the second week.'

It felt like a small victory to Phoebe when she said, 'Assuming people are telling the truth.'

'I just write things down,' Carol said. 'It might be the truth, it might be a lie. I just write it down. I don't suppose you came back to the house during the two weeks, Phoebe?'

'No, I didn't, but I could have been acting in collusion with someone. I thought I'd get that in before you offered it as a possibility, Carol.'

Carol thought that Phoebe Buchanan was too well

put together, too personally curated, to be likeable. She wasn't cold, or bland, but she was a woman who wouldn't be comfortable unless she thought she could exert some control — not necessarily total control — but some control over any given situation. If she hadn't taken the painting, she must now be feeling rather tense. If she had taken it, it might explain this sparring behaviour.

'Most people would be anxious to be eliminated, Phoebe.'

Joyce made a small sound, and when all eyes were on her, she said, 'Phoebe can't bear the idea of being left out of anything. It's an unpleasant vanity she's struggled with all her life.'

It was only Sally who was shocked by the alacrity with which Joyce was prepared to throw her own daughter under a bus. Nothing Joyce said would shock Margaret, who considered her to be unhinged, and Phoebe's long exposure to Joyce had dulled her capacity for surprise. Although this was Carol's first meeting with Joyce, her saintly, floor-licking sister had taught her that sentiment wasn't in the emotional repertoire of the fervently religious. Carol had had enough. It was time to wind things up.

'Phoebe is right about no one being above suspicion. This is far more complicated than it appears on the surface. When the CIB takes over, they are definitely going to want to interview both Sophie White and the premier, as well as everyone else here of course.'

'Oh God,' Gregory said. 'Louisa is going to be furious that she's implicated in this. She's got so much on her plate with the bloody election. Imagine if the press got wind of this?'

'I can see the headline,' Margaret said. '*Premier teaches nude education minister a lesson.*'

'This is you being helpful is it, Mum?'

'I'm just trying to lighten the mood. It was getting a bit dire.'

'It is dire,' Phoebe said sharply. 'Am I the only person who's worried not that the picture's been stolen, but where it's going to end up? When Sophie White hears about this, she's going to love it. She loves controversy. She courts it. She'll go to the press, just to punish Gregory for pulling out of the Archibald and ruining her chance of a win — not that I think that portrait would have stood a snowflake's chance in hell of winning. It's much too skilled a piece of work to win. But what if she has a photograph of it? What if she takes that to the gutter press? This is potentially a public-relations disaster of epic proportions.'

Phoebe's outburst changed the mood in the room. Margaret felt chastened, and asked Carol if the CIB could be dissuaded from interviewing Sophie White. Carol squashed that idea, noting condescendingly that police investigations weren't run on the basis of selective witness interviews.

'As ye sow, so shall ye reap,' Joyce said.

Margaret turned on her.

'You do realise that you're the prime suspect here, don't you, Joyce?'

It didn't seem possible for Joyce's body to become more rigid than it already was, but somehow she achieved an effect of extra rigidity.

'How dare you make such an accusation? How dare you?'

'Mum!' Gregory's voice had a frantic tone to it, which added to the increasingly fraught dynamic in the room. He foolishly thought he might assuage any hurt Joyce was feeling by saying, 'I am sorry, Joyce. I can assure you that I don't condone what my mother has just said.'

Joyce was enlivened by tension, not subdued by it.

'Don't you condone it? I don't see why you wouldn't. I don't see why your wickedness should fall short on that score. A man who brazenly flaunts his private parts is capable of anything.'

Gregory looked confused, as if he simply couldn't grasp the truth of what Phoebe had told him a hundred times — that her mother would never exhibit signs of being reasonable. She wasn't like other people, although this wasn't quite true, Phoebe acknowledged, because she was very like other members in her congregation. Phoebe had met many of them when she was growing up, and the competition to be the most demented was fierce.

'I don't know what you think my son might be capable of, but I might be capable of murder,' Margaret said.

Joyce took a step forward, a movement which resembled a statue coming to life.

'This woman just threatened to kill me,' she said to Carol. 'I insist that you arrest her.'

'Oh relax, Joyce,' Margaret said. 'It's an empty threat. I don't have any silver bullets.'

Sometimes Carol's fascination with conflict overrode her professional objectivity — or even her aversion to the individuals involved. She was interested in the emotional heat between these two women, and although it had nothing to do with the case, she wanted to encourage an explanation for it.

'I'm sensing some antipathy between the two of you. Is this something that might have some bearing on what happened here? Is there something I should know?'

'What you need to know,' Margaret said, 'is that Joyce believes that the world is six thousand years old, a belief that renders her implacably stupid.'

Carol agreed in principle with Margaret's assessment, but her growing dislike of Margaret made her unwilling to give her the satisfaction of feeling supported.

'As a person of faith myself,' she said, 'I think it's unwise to link belief with intelligence.'

'If you believe,' Margaret said slowly, 'that the world is six thousand years old, you are a person of limited intelligence. Faith and intelligence *are* inextricably linked, and if you believe in intelligent design or any of its corollary absurdities, you are a person with the mental acuity of a cephalopod.'

Sally could see that bringing Carol to the house had been a miscalculation, but watching her work had been disappointing and exciting. She couldn't extinguish her attraction to Carol. This burglary situation was unfortunate, and it hadn't gone as well as she'd hoped. Still, if at some stage she could see Carol alone and they could have a proper conversation, perhaps something might eventuate. Her mother's behaviour was typically sabotaging, so she wasn't surprised by it.

'I don't think you should antagonise the police, Mum,' she said, 'and cephalopods are quite intelligent.'

'An octopus opening a jar underwater isn't quite the same as writing *On the Origin of Species* or *Principia Mathematica*, is it?'

Joyce thought she had an ally in Carol, and spoke to her in a confidential tone.

'Margaret has no moral backbone, Carol, and that goes for the rest of them too. Not that I judge them. I'm simply apprising you of their wretched and corrosive lack of belief.'

Carol's pride wouldn't allow her to leave these people with the impression that she shared Joyce's belief about the age of the Earth.

'My job is to remain objective, Joyce. I can't be swayed

by the values, or lack of them, of perpetrators, victims, or witnesses. I am not, I should add, a creationist.'

'That at any rate is a relief,' Margaret said. 'I couldn't engage with a person who thinks the Himalayas popped up five minutes ago. Such a person would be unfit to question a higher primate and wouldn't be capable of coming to a sensible conclusion about anything, let alone this mess. Creationism is an intolerable blight on civilised society. It should be challenged, ridiculed, and dismissed wherever it raises its empty head. A creationist is just somebody in search of the right medication.'

'That's an interesting position,' Carol said, 'but it has no bearing on this situation.'

'Carol's right, Mum. People's religious beliefs aren't anything to do with you or us.'

Margaret wasn't happy with this small act of disloyalty.

'Don't be so naive, Sally. Religion taints everything. If you lived in a world ordered by Joyce, you'd be burned at the stake. Sally is a lesbian, Carol, in case that had escaped your attention.'

'Mum!'

Margaret ploughed on.

'She was rather hoping you were too, Carol, but as a person of faith perhaps you're uncomfortable with any variations on the suffocating norms.'

'What I'm uncomfortable with,' Carol said, 'is your astonishing presumptuousness. Neither my faith nor my sexuality is even remotely any of your business, and I can't believe I have to say this again, but the reason we're here is to sort out the theft of a nude portrait of your son.'

Carol managed to make this sound even more ghastly than it was. She put her notebook back into her bum bag and said, 'I think my work here is done. There is nothing more to be gained, and I see no personal benefit in subjecting myself to further vituperation on my day off. I'll pass my notes on to the CIB. You'll be hearing from them soon.'

Gregory said, 'If I could apologise for my mother's …'

'You may not!' Margaret snapped.

'No apology necessary,' Carol said. 'I understand everyone is a little on edge. Some people deal with that better than others. Will you see me out, Sally?'

They both clattered their way out of the living room, apart from the brief muffling provided by the square of lush carpet.

'That was quite a performance, Mum,' Gregory said. 'It was gratuitously rude and pointless. Carol was doing us a favour. Why did you want to antagonise her?'

Margaret turned to Phoebe.

'Were you impressed with Senior Sergeant Carol whatever-her-last-name-is, Phoebe?'

Before Phoebe could answer, Joyce launched into one her trademark non sequiturs.

'Gregory, the last time we met, the premier gave me

an assurance that her education minister would consider my petition and treat it with respect. I've heard nothing from you.'

Phoebe, with slight weariness, said, 'I believe Louisa's exact words were "the respect it deserves". The ambiguity can't be lost on you, surely.'

Phoebe knew of course that her mother didn't deal in ambiguities. All was certainty. All was clarity. What a pity, Phoebe thought, that it was also wrong.

Joyce was now focused exclusively on her petition.

'The petition has been amended slightly. I was against the amendments, but I'm not an inflexible person, so I agreed to it. We are *not* now demanding that Christian doctrine be taught in Islamic schools. We do not wish to unleash a campaign of bombing.'

Gregory felt compelled to challenge this.

'Joyce, that is a deeply offensive and ignorant remark.'

With indifferent sangfroid, Joyce said, 'I don't think you are in a position to declare what is and what is not offensive. A man who exposes himself to the world is no one's idea of a moral bellwether.'

The clatter of Sally's shoes announced her return.

'You were a long time saying goodbye to Miss Marple,' Margaret said. 'She wasn't patting you down, was she?'

Sally harboured a suspicion that her mother suppressed her homophobia and that her energetic celebration of lesbianism, especially Sally's lesbianism, was a smokescreen. This was merely a suspicion, but Margaret's overt disapproval of Carol did nothing to ease it.

'I admit,' Sally said, 'that that didn't go as well as I'd hoped it would, but it wasn't all bad. We're going out for dinner. Tonight.'

She smiled at her mother.

When Carol left the Buchanan house, the first thing she did, after making her date with Sally, was ring the CIB and ask to be put through to Detective Sergeant Jack Craig. She disliked Jack Craig, and she now disliked Gregory Buchanan, so bringing them together seemed like a good idea. Her feelings about Jack Craig had something to do with an entirely unreasonable distrust of people whose first name and last name were interchangeable. She thought this could only be the result of generational laziness and lack of imagination. Surely at some point, *someone* in the family would have recognised the confusion that might arise from having a surname that was also a first name, and done something about it.

It wasn't just his name, though. Jack Craig was an oaf. He wasn't big-bellied or poorly shaven or red in the face, but Carol thought that this version of Jack Craig was inside him, struggling to get out. She'd worked with him, briefly, so she knew that there was a long list of things he despised. At the top of this list were left-leaning politicians and arty wankers. He'd hate Gregory Buchanan on sight, and hate even more the awful obligation to behave professionally. He was an oaf, but he wasn't a moron. Getting on the wrong side of a minister in government might, at some later date, scupper his ambition to be the police commissioner — an ambition he'd drunkenly expressed to a gobsmacked Carol after work one day. She'd been gobsmacked because the distance between his abilities and his self-belief was vast.

It was serendipitous that the Buchanan house was within Jack Craig's investigative bailiwick, and the value of the missing painting meant that the investigation fell to the plain-clothes boys and girls, rather than uniform.

'Jack,' she said, 'I've got a job that requires sensitive handling, so naturally I thought of you.'

Craig was never sure when Carol was taking the piss. No one had ever accused him of being sensitive before, and it wasn't a quality he particularly admired. Still, women were suckers for sensitive men, apparently, so perhaps Carol was responding to a quality he wasn't aware he had — and that had to be flattering, right?

'Fill me in, Caz.'

Carol loathed being called Caz, and it sounded especially revolting coming out of Craig's mouth. She outlined the details of the case but withheld the crucial nugget that the missing painting wasn't just a portrait, but a nude portrait. She wanted Jack to discover that for himself, in front of the family. She stressed that Gregory Buchanan was a minister on the rise, knowing that this would discourage Craig from handballing the case to another officer.

'The thing is, Jack, this will require a little discretion. When a painting of a pollie goes missing, there might be more to it than meets the eye.'

Craig wasn't sure what this might mean, but he was sufficiently intrigued to decide on the spot that he'd make the initial visit to the Buchanans alone. If there were any kudos to be had in the solving of this case, he didn't want to share them. How hard could it be to find a huge fucking painting? He had a network of low-lifes and scumbags all over the city. If anyone tried to shift this thing in a pub, he'd hear about it.

Carol ended the phone call with a deep sense of satisfaction.

Sally's news that she was going out to dinner with Carol Hinton wasn't met with unalloyed joy by her mother.

'Try to wear natural fibres,' Margaret said. 'The two of you in a lycra clinch could start a fire.'

Before Sally could respond, the doorbell rang and gave each of them a jolt.

'Nancy Drew must have forgotten something,' Margaret said.

As Gregory moved towards the door, he said, 'It might be Louisa.'

Phoebe put her hands on her belly as if to reassure the fetus that life wasn't usually this chaotic or stressful.

'This is turning into a fiasco,' she said, 'and in the end it's a fiasco of Gregory's own making. If that wretched Sophie White hadn't painted that hideous portrait, everything would be just fine.'

When Sophie White entered the room, she did so in time to hear herself described as 'wretched', although she didn't react in any way. It might have been difficult regardless to discern a reaction on her face. She was a slight woman in her early forties, with a fierce, immobile little face, which was thin and slightly avian in its incapacity to register subtle shifts of emotion. Her resting expression was stern. Her active expression was stern. If she was unconscious, she looked stern. Her skin was unlined, having rarely been subjected to the rigours of smiling. Her lips were barely there, and she wasn't given to pursing them. They remained stiffly parallel beneath her small, shapely nose. Her nose was the feature on her face that received the most exercise. Her nostrils weren't large, but constant flaring of them had widened them over time.

'Ah,' Gregory said, 'this is Sophie White. Sophie, this is my wife …'

'I'm not here to meet people or to make new friends. I don't care who any of these people are. I'm here for one reason and one reason only — to prevent a travesty from occurring.'

No one found this level of brutal honesty bracing. On the other hand, no one was intimidated by it either. If asked, the consensus would have been that Sophie White was rude, not formidable. People with appalling manners often confused the two. It made no material difference to Joyce's opinion of her. Joyce thought of her as the woman who had gazed upon Gregory's nakedness. Sophie White was, therefore, the Whore of Babylon, and as such only vileness could issue forth from her mouth.

'You're in no danger of making friends here, my dear,' Margaret said.

Although she didn't approve of Sophie's opening gambit, Sally was willing to engage with her, because she really did believe that Sophie White was an important artist. Sally retained a romantic notion that great talent excused bad behaviour. She'd held on to this notion because she'd never experienced full-blown diva behaviour from anyone. In the spirit of conciliation, she put out her hand for Sophie to shake.

'Sophie, I'm Sally. Gregory's sister.'

Sophie looked at the proffered hand and left it

unattended to. Sally withdrew it, and Phoebe noticed the blush that rose in her cheeks. Sally's embarrassment caused Phoebe's dislike of Sophie White to transmute into loathing.

'I'm Gregory's wife, Phoebe. If you're here to try to get him to change his mind, you're wasting your time.'

'I understand that your husband's body offends you. I call that sad.'

'My husband's body does not offend me. Your rendering of it does. Mightily.'

'It isn't even a question of whether it's a good, bad, or indifferent painting,' Margaret said. 'That is no longer the point.'

Sophie wasn't paying any attention to what was being said. She was staring at Gregory, and there was very little admiration in the stare. Her gaze was diverted when Joyce spat out a savage, 'It's an obscene painting.'

Gregory looked like he was about to say something, but Joyce stopped him. 'I don't wish to be introduced, Gregory. I don't want my name in this creature's mouth.'

This singular locution pulled everyone up short, and provided a brief, shocked respite from argument.

'Please,' Gregory finally said, 'can we all try to be calm and civil?'

Barely had he said this before something broke inside him and took with it his own calm and civility. 'I'd appreciate it, Joyce,' he said sharply, 'if you could curb your natural tendency towards egregious rudeness.'

There was another moment of shocked silence.

'Oh how quickly the mask slips,' Joyce said. 'How *quickly* it slips.'

'I think you deserve an apology, Sophie, for this hostile reception.' Because he was looking at Sophie, Gregory didn't see the expression of horror that crossed Phoebe's and Margaret's faces. Sophie didn't notice it either, not that it would have bothered her if she had.

'You don't need to protect me from my critics, Gregory.' She waved her hand in Joyce's direction. 'I like the fact that this woman despises my work. The idea of producing anything that pleased her makes me want to …' She thought about how to end this sentence and settled on '… makes me want to vomit.'

'A sensation you're quite happy to excite in others,' said Phoebe.

'I feed on hostility. I breathe it like oxygen.'

This wasn't empty bravura. Sophie had distrusted compliments since childhood. They'd always been hard-won, and when they were given she found them only briefly satisfying, like sugar. She was, anyway, and always had been, a difficult person to compliment. She'd been a surly child, not much given to expressions of joy. She'd been a mystery to her parents, who'd adopted her as a baby. They were an uncomplicated couple who worried constantly that they must be doing something wrong. They started to believe that their parenting was amateurish, as if there were a professional version and they lacked the skills to achieve it. Sophie didn't despise her parents — that would have required an emotional commitment that she wasn't prepared to give. She thought them dull, suburban, and unimaginative, which they indisputably were. The fact that they loved her ought to have trumped these shortcomings, but love was a kind of compliment, so it went unappreciated and undervalued.

She'd shown an impressive facility for drawing from a very young age, and by twelve it had become clear that this was more than a facility: it was a talent. Her parents nurtured this talent (Sophie would have rejected the word 'nurtured' as cloying) by providing her with materials, and with 'How to Draw' and 'How to Paint' books. She found these books laughable and insulting, and told her parents that what she needed was life-drawing classes. At twelve years old, they thought her too young to be exposed to naked bodies. This infuriated her, and she harassed them almost every day until her fifteenth birthday.

She left home at seventeen. She was fierce about her work. She was fierce about everything. She went through lovers as frequently as she went through tubes of paint. Her longest relationship lasted two tubes of Thalo blue, and Thalo blue was regularly used in her palette. She became something of an enfant terrible, specialising in portraits that were as excoriating as Lucian Freud's. When a critic made this comparison, Sophie was enraged, believing that her art had no antecedents.

She softened her style and began to acquire a reputation as a reliable and quite conservative portraitist. Her sitters rarely enjoyed the experience — she was sour and uncommunicative — but they went away with a picture they were happy to pay her for. She was aware that she was no longer considered daring, and whenever this bothered her she checked her bank balance and the bothersome sensation went away.

At some point, she decided that she had to win the Archibald Prize. There were things about the Archibald that she held in contempt. How, over the span of one hundred years of competition, had only ten women taken the main prize; and how had only sixteen women been the subjects of winning entries? She'd win this fucking prize if it was the last thing she did.

In her studio, one wall had been graffitied by her, in beautiful copperplate, with a headline from *The Australian Women's Weekly* celebrating Nora Heysen's win in 1938, the first by a woman: *Girl Painter Who Won Art Prize is also Good Cook*. Underneath this was Max Meldrum's dictum in response to her win that, *If I were a woman I would certainly prefer raising a healthy family to a career in art. I believe that such a life is unnatural and impossible for a woman.* She read these every day.

She'd entered the Archibald three times, been selected each time, and won the packers' prize once, for a portrait of a rugby player in his underwear. Each time, she'd been beaten by, in her view, a vastly inferior portrait. She'd been told privately that although her work was admired, it was thought to be 'safe', and 'safe' didn't cause a stir — and after all, the Archibald wasn't really about art. It was about the 'stir'.

When Gregory Buchanan had walked into her studio, she'd sized him up as susceptible to flattery and to being convinced that he was that rare thing, a politician who was willing to take chances, to be daring, to challenge the complacency of the mainstream. It had been surprisingly easy to get him to take his clothes off. He'd bought her line about subverting the long history of the male gaze. They talked about the predictably eccentric taste of the Archibald judges and agreed that the judges were so blind to real talent that if John Singer Sargent had been alive today, his chances of winning would be minimal. But what, Sophie had said, what if they were presented with a portrait of a public figure painted with all the bravura and solid technique of a Sargent, but with that figure frankly, confidently, and shockingly naked? Gregory, to Sophie's surprise, and disdain, had fallen for it.

'Things are tense here, Sophie,' Gregory said, 'because your portrait, which as you know, I love, your portrait …'

'My portrait is going to hang in the Archibald. Nothing is more certain than that.'

With mock regret, Margaret said, 'There's no such

thing as certainty, as you're about to find out.'

'As I'm the one guiding my certainty, I think I'm in a better position than you to judge that.'

'You and Joyce here have a lot in common. Joyce thinks faith is all that matters, and you think art is all that matters. You're both addicted to self-indulgent proselytising.'

'Faith *is* everything,' Joyce said.

'*Art* is everything,' Sophie said at a lower but more dangerous pitch.

'My husband's career is what matters here, not intellectual theorising.'

'Oh Christ,' Sophie said. 'A surrendered wife.'

Phoebe allowed this gibe to pass her by. It was a ludicrous thing to say.

'That's just glib,' she said. 'Politics needs people with integrity, and Gregory has integrity — not that you gave him any in your portrait. That was the most offensive thing about it, not the nudity. You made him look grasping. The whole portrait was a lie.'

Sophie scoffed.

'The art will always have more integrity than the sitter. The sitter is always compromised in some way. The art will tell the truth. The sitter's ego will always get in the way of him telling the truth.'

'How can the art have integrity if the artist has none? You took advantage of Gregory's vanity, and you know perfectly well that if that picture is shown publicly, he will lose his seat in this election. There's nothing surer than that.'

A range of emotions had crossed Gregory's face during this exchange.

'He knew exactly what he was doing when he posed for me.'

'Abomination,' said Joyce.

'And I celebrated his courage, wrongly as it turns out. If you want to talk about integrity, what do you say about a man who goes back on his word? I'd say he's a man whose word is worth nothing. A politician, in fact.'

Gregory had calmed himself down sufficiently to say, 'Would you stop arguing about me as if I'm not in the room?' He patted the air in front of him as if this might settle disruptive vibrations. 'Sophie, perhaps you don't know, although I did think I told you, that I've been appointed minister for education, and you can understand that that portfolio and your portrait of me are not a good fit.'

Sophie curled her almost non-existent lips.

'It's a better fit than the alternative, believe me.'

There was silence for a moment.

'What's that supposed to mean?' Margaret said. 'That sounds like a threat.'

Looking directly at Gregory, Sophie said, 'That is a threat.'

'Whatever you're threatening to do, Sophie,' Phoebe said, 'it's pointless. Even if Gregory wanted to, he couldn't put the painting in the Archibald. It's gone.'

'It's been stolen,' Gregory said quickly, in case Sophie thought it had been destroyed.

Everyone waited for her reaction. For a moment there was nothing, and then a very rare thing happened. She laughed. It wasn't a hearty laugh. It was more of a gurgle, as if her body were trying to accommodate an unfamiliar physical response.

'Oh,' she said, 'I can see why you entered politics. I saw it when I painted you. Stolen? Please. Pull the other one.'

Sally, who, despite everything that had transpired in the last few minutes, hadn't been inoculated against Sophie's personality, sought to provide her with some kind of reassurance.

'No, really, Sophie. It has been stolen, from right off the wall. It was right over there, in the dining room, and when Phoebe and Gregory came back from the country, it wasn't there anymore. You can see the empty frame. Let me show you.'

With great reluctance, Sophie relaxed her rigid stance and went with Sally to the dining room. She examined the fallen frame and confirmed that the canvas had indeed been cut free.

'How very convenient,' she said. 'A vandal has been here. Re-stretching it will involve some paint loss around the edges. I don't construct my pictures with vandalism in mind.'

Gregory joined them.

'Did you do this?' Sophie asked savagely.

'Certainly not, and as to its being convenient, it couldn't in fact be more inconvenient. Having definitely decided — and again, I'm sorry — having decided that discretion was the better part of valour in this instance, I've now lost control of the painting. Whoever's taken it might use it to blackmail me, or just to embarrass me and the government. They might release it to the press, and that will be the end of my career in parliament.'

Sophie's basilisk expression remained unchanged although her tone was unambiguously hostile.

'Bluff and double bluff. I'm not as gullible as the people who vote for you, Gregory. If you think you can make your commitment to me go away by staging a clumsy theft, and by damaging my work in the process, you need to have a quick rethink.'

She walked up to Gregory and poked him hard in the chest, an act that was so sudden that it appeared more violent than it was.

'I'll give you twenty-four hours,' she said. She walked back into the living room, and it was clear that she was on her way out.

'Twenty-four hours,' she repeated.

'Twenty-four hours to do what?' Phoebe asked.

'To recover the painting. I'm confident that you won't need a miracle.'

Once again, Sally attempted reassurance.

'It *is* a real theft, Sophie. It's been reported to the police. They've been here. They've taken notes.' The plural pronoun wasn't quite accurate, but Sally thought it lent credence to the theft.

'I can see for myself that the picture's been taken from the frame. I can also see a roomful of people who want it to remain gone. Why would anyone outside this family break in and steal my painting and, I presume, only my painting?'

'It's certainly a puzzle why anyone would want it,' Phoebe said.

'But not such a puzzle as to why they might want to get rid of it.'

If no one had said anything, Sophie might have left at this point, but Margaret couldn't help herself.

'We don't want it hung in the Archibald. That's a long way from wanting to destroy it. We're not barbarians.'

Joyce reiterated her position on this.

'I would destroy it without hesitation. God doesn't offer dispensations to produce pornography just because he's given you the ability to draw.'

Sophie's second attempt at a laugh ended in little more than a tiny, strangled sound.

'You think I should stick to puppies and kittens,' she said.

Joyce offered Sophie an unblinking stare.

'I think you should get down on your hands and

knees and beg forgiveness for the sordid corruption of your God-given talent.'

As Joyce was speaking, Sophie reached into her back pocket and produced a mobile phone. She held it in front of Joyce and took a photograph.

'Superb,' she said. 'Truly superb.'

Joyce raised her hands to her chest.

'What did you just do?'

'I just photographed madness, and I can't wait to paint it. I don't think madness should be wearing clothes, though. I can see what you look like naked, and that's how I'll paint you. It won't be flattering. Just looking at your general shape, I'm assuming the worst.'

Joyce wasn't to be goaded. Nevertheless, Gregory thought Sophie's suggestion was sufficiently shocking to demand that he say something.

'You can't come into my house and point your camera at people. I'm sorry, but I'm going to have to ask you to leave.'

'You needn't rush to my defence, Gregory. I hope this, this ... whatever she is, looks long and hard into my face. She may find the light of salvation there.'

Gregory's irritation and frustration broke through.

'I'm not defending you, Joyce. I consider it an abuse of *our* hospitality.' He straightened up in a slightly comical assertion of dignity. 'I'll keep you informed of the progress of the police investigation of course, but I have to reiterate that even if the painting is recovered, it won't be hanging in the Archibald.'

'I couldn't give a flying fuck about the police investigation, or even if one exists. What I care about, Gregory, is your commitment to me and to my art.' Her voice began to rise. 'That picture will win. It's my turn! And it's my best work.'

'Well, thank you,' Gregory said.

'What? Why are you thanking me? What's it got to do with you?'

'I'm thanking you because I'm happy that you're pleased with our collaboration and that that collaboration resulted in your best work. It doesn't, however, change anything.'

Sophie couldn't let the assertion that her work was in any way a collaboration go unchallenged.

'I have no idea what you mean by collaboration.'

'Artist and subject.'

Insofar as Sophie's face was capable of registering it, she registered astonishment.

'It's a great picture because I painted it, not because you stripped off and posed for it. If the Archibald accepted a cane toad as a subject, I'd have painted one.'

Gregory, emboldened by that glimpse of petulance — it made Sophie less intimidating — said, 'Be that as it may, the fact of the matter is, and let me be perfectly clear on this, the subject exists without the artist, the artist doesn't exist without the subject.'

Phoebe, Margaret, and Sally looked at Gregory, and

what each felt, in varying degrees, was admiration. Was what he'd said banal, or profound? No one was sure.

Sophie had no doubts on this count.

'Are you taking credit for my work?'

Gregory's rush of confidence continued.

'You painted what you saw and what you felt, and I was unarguably at the heart of both responses. If the picture were ever to be exhibited publicly, I hope you don't think I'd be silent about my part in its creation, and its success as a work of art.'

Sophie folded her arms, and unfolded them, not wishing to give the impression of defensiveness. She knew, however, something that no one else in the room knew. She knew that she had an ace up her sleeve, a deadly arrow in her quiver, a dumdum bullet in the chamber of her gun. So her narrow face shifted in the approximation of a smile.

'I see,' she said. 'Obviously I underestimated the vast geography of your ego. I'd need sat nav to find my way around it. Well I can work with that because I know it will work in my favour.'

A vague sense of dread descended on the room.

'I hadn't planned on doing this now. I was going to send you a text later.'

Gregory's puzzlement was obvious. Sophie took out her phone and took a moment to find whatever it was she looking for.

'Sent,' she said, and put her phone away. 'I suggest

you check your email, and we'll see how committed you really are to your importance in the artistic process.'

Phoebe had a very bad feeling about where this was going.

'What do you mean?' she asked.

'You're in PR, I believe, so PR the shit out of this, if you can. I said you had twenty-four hours to make my picture reappear, and we all know that there'll be no miracle involved in that, don't we?'

'It was stolen!' Gregory said. 'Of course it will take a miracle. It's out of our hands.'

'Check your email. Go ahead.'

Gregory went upstairs to get his laptop. He'd normally just check his emails on his phone, but fetching the laptop provided him with a breather. He needed just a minute or two away from everyone, and besides, whatever Sophie had sent through would be seen to better advantage on his laptop screen. Just as he picked up the computer, his phone rang. It was a police detective, Jack Craig, and being thoroughly distracted Gregory agreed that the man could come round to the house immediately. When Gregory came back downstairs with his laptop, he saw that no one had moved an inch or spoken a word. He flipped it open and turned it on.

'Okay, it's here,' he said, and clicked on the attachment in the email message. The screen was filled with what looked like the original portrait. 'You made a copy. It looks like a straight copy, or is it just a photograph of the original?'

Margaret, Phoebe, and Sally moved to where they could see the image. It was a large file, and Gregory hadn't chosen the 'fit in window' option, so what was visible was his head and shoulders. Unexpectedly, Joyce reminded everyone that she was still in the room.

'When you're finished with that computer, Gregory, you'll notice, when you read it, that we've requested the removal of laptops from schools. They are pornography vectors, nothing more.'

In grimly measured tones and still staring at the screen, Gregory said, 'You shouldn't be too optimistic about the success of your petition, Joyce.'

'We are not optimistic. We are certain. We are prayerful.'

'Prayer won't convince the government to turn the clock back six hundred years.'

'We shall see. We shall see.'

Joyce was on the periphery of everyone's interest. They were looking intently at the image on the screen.

'It looks the same to me,' Phoebe said. 'Scroll down.'

Gregory began to scroll down slowly.

Sophie remained expressionless.

The scrolling stopped.

'Oh,' said Phoebe.

'Oh,' said Margaret.

'Oh,' said Sally.

'Oh no,' said Gregory.

'What has happened?' asked Joyce, and internally berated herself for showing any interest.

'Look for yourself, Joyce,' said Margaret.

'I wouldn't sully my sight.'

Sally thought it was important to sully some aspect of Joyce, so she said, 'It's an identical portrait, Joyce, in every detail, except for one. Gregory's penis is now the size of an acorn.'

'You need to zoom in for a nice surprise,' Sophie said.

Reluctantly, Gregory did so.

Margaret's hand went involuntarily to her mouth.

'Oh my giddy aunt. There's a swastika tattooed on the end of your … member. When did you have that done? And why?'

'For God's sake, Mum! I don't have any tattoos, and I certainly don't have one there!'

Sophie cleared her throat.

'My work here is done. I'll be releasing *this* portrait to the press as my entry in the Archibald Prize — and I have your signed permission to do so, which will of course act as your endorsement that this is an accurate portrayal of you and one with which you are comfortable. This *will* happen unless the original resurfaces. I'll be more than happy to acknowledge your courage and determination to make our collaboration a success. An artist is nothing, after all, without a subject.'

She turned on her heel and left, not waiting to be escorted out. Sally hurried after her, which startled Margaret.

'If she comes back with that monster's phone number, I'll disown her.'

Gregory closed the lid of his computer. He was agitated. He wouldn't have admitted it, but some of that agitation was directed at himself. He wanted to believe in the integrity of his decision to be painted by Sophie White, but his courage was beginning to look like folly. Yet owning up to this now was out of the question. He channelled his frustration towards the absent Sally.

'Sally was quite taken with Sophie White, wasn't she?'

'Not that I noticed,' Phoebe said.

'I take no pleasure in saying it,' Margaret said, 'but the fact is, Sally is a star-fucker.'

Joyce winced, which pleased Margaret.

'She reads *Hello!* magazine, Joyce.'

'Your mouth and your mind are sewers emptying into your soul.'

The words were flung into the room, and as Sally returned she assumed she was included in their net.

'Well?' Margaret snapped at Sally.

'Well what?'

'Whose side are you on?'

There was nasty edge to the question that puzzled Sally.

'I'm on the side of art. That puts me on Gregory's side, doesn't it?'

Gregory's exasperation was now so generalised that Sally was subsumed into it. He rarely quarrelled with her, but he wanted to quarrel with her now.

'Sophie White is trying to blackmail and humiliate me, Sally! Her picture is so lifelike that people who see it will assume that I have a tiny, tattooed cock!'

Trying to minimise the I-told-you-so quality in her voice, Phoebe said, 'She's clever. I'll give her that. She's using your vanity to blackmail you.'

'Call her bluff,' Sally said. 'No one cares about the size of your dick.'

Gregory looked at her with an expression that suggested he couldn't believe what she'd said.

'*I* care. How can I stand up in parliament when all those opposition arseholes think they know what's behind my fly and that it's not very much?'

This was a level of male panic that none of the women in the room had thought about seriously.

'Men and their dicks,' Sally said. 'It's so pathetic.'

Gregory's temper flared.

'She's painted a swastika on my knob, Sally!'

'As ye sow, so shall ye reap,' Joyce said.

'That's all very well, Joyce, but it isn't very helpful. What am I going to do?'

This last was addressed to everyone, but it was Joyce who answered.

'Wicked, wanton vanity. God will not be mocked, and he will exact a price.'

It is a testament to the stress that Gregory was experiencing that he abandoned his long-held policy of not attacking his mother-in-law.

'Joyce,' Gregory said, 'I have tried over several years now to accept the tenets of your peculiar faith as being of great importance to you. I have always thought that you should be free to enjoy them without interference. I am aware that I have not enjoyed a similar indulgence from you. Nevertheless, I have borne your ignorance and intolerance with what I hope was equanimity and which I'm sure you saw as weakness. However, I am not a bottomless reservoir of patience, and the well has now run dry. Bone dry. I will *not* be presenting your petition to the premier, or to cabinet. It's an absurd and embarrassing document. The world has already lived through the eleventh century, and repeating the experience is pointless.'

Gregory delivered this speech with disciplined control, and it reminded his listeners why he was considered a talented parliamentary performer. Joyce, however, was unfazed. She was deaf to eloquence.

Under normal circumstances, Jack Craig would have delayed beginning a new case, but the Buchanan theft was different. There might be something in it for him, career-wise.

Before setting out for the house, he googled Gregory Buchanan. He discovered that Gregory was on the wrong side of the House; he was the kind of politician Jack Craig would never vote for. He checked what the man looked like on Google Images and thought he looked like a school prefect. He was tall and lean with good hair and good teeth. Buchanan was married. There was a picture of him at some do with his wife, whose name was Phoebe. Of course it was.

His detestation of Gregory began to run away with him, and he checked himself with the reminder, not that Gregory had been the victim of a crime and deserved sympathy, but that he was a minister in a sitting government and this could be advantageous to Jack. He reminded himself of this again as he knocked on Gregory's expensive-looking door. He then noticed the doorbell and rang it for good measure.

The intrusion of the doorbell prevented Gregory from continuing his attack on Joyce.

'That will be Detective Jack Craig reporting for duty,' he said. 'I think that's what he said his name was. He said he'd be here within a few minutes. Could this actually be a good sign?'

'I hope he's wearing a suit,' Margaret said. 'I've had my fill of lycra for one day.'

'Before I get the door, can we agree that this

detective needs to be told about the theft but not about Sophie White's blackmail? That's a separate issue.'

Without waiting to hear whether anybody agreed with this, Gregory answered the door. Detective Sergeant Jack Craig introduced himself, and Gregory brought him into the living room, where he was surprised to find four women. He'd half-hoped that the premier might be there. What was her name? Louisa somebody. He wasn't good at politician's surnames. He knew them mostly by the epithets he gave them, if he knew them at all. He knew Louisa Wetherly as 'that fuckhead'. This was based solely on the fact that he'd voted against her in the last election. That she'd won the election, in spite of his precious vote, made him feel that that vote had been disregarded. Ipso facto, she was a fuckhead.

'This is Detective Senior Sergeant Jack Craig,' Gregory said, giving him a promotion, which Jack liked the sound of and which he didn't correct. It also shifted his view of Gregory slightly. Maybe he wasn't such a wanker after all.

Gregory made the introductions, and Jack immediately forgot who everyone was. There was a woman with a decent figure squeezed into lycra, which Jack appreciated. Maybe he'd get her number and give her a ring. He didn't do suave, but being a detective was sexy, right?

'Thanks for coming so quickly,' Gregory said. 'We really appreciate it.'

Jack nodded and furrowed his brow, because police work was a brow-furrowingly serious business.

'Sergeant Hinton has briefed me about what happened here. A very valuable work of art has gone missing, is that right?'

Everyone's patience had been exhausted by Carol's questioning and Sophie White's belligerence, and no one was looking forward to going through it all over again. Margaret said, 'We've all had enough for one day of looking at, talking about, and worrying about my son's penis.'

There had been many occasions in Jack Craig's life when he'd been flummoxed — he was flummox-prone — but this one took the biscuit, and his face showed it.

'You said Sergeant Hinton briefed you,' Margaret said, 'so you must realise that this is all about Gregory's penis and who gets to see it and who doesn't.'

Jack had never been adept at joining dots and he couldn't make a connection between this alarming talk about Gregory's private parts and the stolen work of art. Is this what Carol had meant about sensitivity and discretion? Had Gregory Buchanan, the education minister, been exposing himself? He examined Gregory more closely and thought, yeah, he looks like a flasher.

'Well now,' he said. 'This is delicate. I don't know if we can sweep indecent exposure under the carpet. It's a serious offence. There weren't any kiddies involved, were there? Because if there were, I'd have to hand this on to the sexual-crimes unit.'

'What are you talking about?' Gregory asked. 'What did Sergeant Hinton tell you?'

'She said a painting was stolen. She didn't mention this other business of you dropping your duds.'

Joyce laughed. It was a strangled laugh because, in common with Sophie White, laughter wasn't a normal part of her vocal range.

Gregory said, 'I think you've got the wrong end of the stick, inspector. I haven't been dropping my duds, to use your ghastly expression, and I certainly haven't been doing it in front of children. I mean, for God's sake.'

Jack Craig was all at sea.

'The reason you're here, inspector, is because a painting has indeed been stolen, and that's the only reason you're here.'

Impatient for Gregory to get to the point, Phoebe said, 'The painting is a nude portrait of Gregory. Why do you always bury the lead when talking about this, Gregory?'

Gregory was feeling under siege, and to escape the living room he suggested that Jack accompany him to the scene of the crime.

The two of them stood before the empty frame.

'The damage to the plaster has nothing to do with the theft, but the fact that the painting was leaning against the wall made it easier for the thief to cut the canvas from the frame.'

'It filled that whole frame, Gregory?'

'It's a full-length portrait, slightly larger than life-size.'

'Nothing wrong with adding an extra inch or two.'

How has this oaf risen through the ranks, Gregory thought?

'Are you wearing anything in this picture, Gregory?'

'Chanel No. 5,' Gregory said snippily, expecting Jack to get the Marilyn Monroe reference. He didn't, and his opinion of Gregory sank even lower as he now supposed that the education minister wore a sheila's perfume.

'Any distinguishing features?'

Between clenched teeth Gregory said, 'My face.'

'I don't suppose you've got a photo of this painting. That'd be helpful.'

'No. What other information do you need? I presume Carol, Sergeant Hinton, passed her notes on to you.'

'She summarised them, so I'm up to speed. This is just a preliminary visit you understand. What we need to do, Gregory, is sort out who would want a picture of you in the altogether. Motive. That's what we're after. A motive.'

Not wishing to encourage him, Gregory said simply, 'Yes.'

'Who benefits, Gregory? The person who benefits is our thief. Any ideas?'

'As far as I can see, no one benefits.'

Jack had a vague inkling that there might be more to this crime than met the eye, but he'd need time to think about it. He wasn't a quick thinker. There was something murky here, though.

'Why did you want to be painted in the nuddy, Gregory?'

'That isn't relevant, is it? I don't want to discuss art with you. I'd just like you to find the painting.'

Jack hated being spoken to like this, as if he were a poorly qualified tradesman. He suddenly couldn't care less about Gregory Buchanan or his bloody awful portrait. It had to be bloody awful: it was a picture of a bloke with his balls on display. Only his dream of being the police commissioner stopped him from telling this perfume-wearing, pants-dropping, cock-out excuse for a real man what he really thought of him.

'I think I've got all I need for the moment,' he said carefully, worried that his tone might give him away. It did give him away, and Gregory was caught in an awful paradox. He wanted Jack Craig gone, but he also wanted him to at least make a feint at doing his job.

'Will you be conducting any interviews before you leave?'

'I don't think so. Not at this stage.'

'What sort of investigative strategies will you put in place?'

'The thing is, Gregory, this picture of you is going to be hard to shift on the pub circuit. Whoever took it didn't think it through. You can't just rock up to a bar and unfurl it for a potential client, can you?'

Gregory couldn't quite believe what he was hearing. 'This is a painting, not a flat-screen TV,' he said.

Jack tried very hard not to be condescending. 'In my experience, Gregory, most burgled items find their way into pubs. I've seen whole dining suites change hands in a pub lounge.'

Gregory had no response to this, which Jack took as an acknowledgement of his greater experience of criminal behaviour. With this boost to his ego, he decided to ask a few questions after all. He was prepared to delay his departure just to press home what he saw as an advantage. He hadn't detected Gregory's urgent wish to have him leave, because detection was only his job description, not his skill.

'Just before I go, Gregory,' he said, attempting an homage to Colombo's celebrated last-minute, devastating questions. 'Who do you think took this painting?'

Gregory's patience was in tatters.

'If I knew that, you wouldn't be here.'

'You'll need to clarify that, Gregory.'

'I believe the traditional role of the detective is to find the solution to a crime that is not apparent to the victims of that crime.'

Even Jack Craig couldn't fail correctly to interpret Gregory's tone.

'Do you have any enemies?'

'Of course I have enemies. I'm a politician. The opposition are not fans.'

In what he thought was a piercing insight, Jack said, 'So if one of your enemies got hold of this nudie painting, he could use it against you.'

'Precisely,' Gregory said. 'You've stumbled on the real issue here.'

Jack nodded sagely.

'This might be bigger than Ben Hur, Gregory.'

In a split second, Jack made the decision that he wanted nothing more to do with this case. He'd definitely pass it on to someone else. He'd realised that he might be required to ask awkward questions of members of the opposition. They were the opposition now, but oppositions had a record of becoming governments, and he didn't want any of them remembering that he'd once accused them of a crime by questioning them as if they were legitimate suspects.

'Cut.'

'What?'

'Cut from the frame.' Jack thought that this Holmesian aperçu would leave a good impression, and rather than risk compromising it with further embellishments, he added, 'I'll be off. I'll certainly be in touch when I've put a team together.'

One of these nongs was bad enough, Gregory thought, a whole team of them was unthinkable. He accepted the abruptness of Jack Craig's decision to leave, without demur.

In the living room, the four women were in the same positions they'd been in a couple of minutes earlier. It was strange tableau that Jack Craig neither noticed nor wondered about. Indeed, it was as if the room were empty. He simply passed through without even a desultory farewell. It was his intention never to see any of these people again. As soon as he got back to the office, he'd unload this case, and do his best Pontius Pilate.

'What a frightful person,' Margaret said.

'I'm frankly amazed that any crimes get solved,' Gregory said. 'It must be true that most criminals have the IQ of a tree stump. Now, where were we?'

Joyce sniffed.

'We were discussing my petition.'

'The petition will go nowhere, Joyce. I have explained this to you already. I can't make it any clearer.'

Joyce waited, just for a moment, and it seemed to Phoebe that she was reloading.

'You *will* present the petition to the premier, and you *will* speak strongly in its favour on the floor of the House.'

There was something in Joyce's voice that Phoebe recognised. There was chilly certainty that could only mean that she had something up her sleeve.

'Why would Gregory do that?' she asked quietly.

'Because he finds himself on the horns of a dilemma, and because I find myself with the means to pry him loose.'

# Part
# THREE

It took a moment for the implication of what Joyce had said to sink in, and when it did it was Margaret who couldn't contain her outrage.

'I knew it! I knew it! All that pious bullshit about not touching the vile object. I said right at the beginning that it was you. *You* took it, and you lied through your teeth about it. Hypocrite!'

Joyce was triumphantly calm.

'I didn't touch it.' She paused. 'I wore gloves, and while I took it out of the frame, I didn't take it out of the house. I stole nothing.'

'Mum, what did you think you were doing?'

'I *knew* what I was doing. I was doing God's work.'

'You were committing a crime!'

'It was more of a spiritual intervention. And what is the crime? Rearranging your furnishings?'

Joyce was rarely guilty of a witticism. It was a measure of how pleased she was with herself that she was able to deliver this one. Under the present circumstances, it went unappreciated.

Between gritted teeth, Phoebe said, 'Where is it?'

The doorbell rang and everyone jumped.

'That will be Louisa,' Gregory said. 'Unless it's another one of your surprises, Joyce.'

Joyce smiled benignly, or maliciously, depending on your point of view. Gregory left to answer the door.

'Wow,' Sally said. 'I'd make a crap detective. I was sure that Gregory had taken it himself so he wouldn't have to back down about the Archibald.'

'Oh, I knew it was Joyce,' Margaret said, 'but the way you were sucking up to Sophie White, I half-thought that you and she were in cahoots.'

'Oh well thank you very much! It's so reassuring to get a big vote of confidence from my own mother. What possible motive would Sophie White have for taking her own portrait?'

Margaret shrugged.

'Blackmail, darling. Agree to hang the original or I'll hang the copy. As it turns out, the blackmail idea is the same, but she has an unexpected accomplice.'

She looked at Joyce.

'I'm assuming you're an accidental accomplice. Unless of course you and Sophie White …'

Joyce snorted.

'I'd rather sup with the devil than have anything to do with that strumpet,' she said.

'Where is the painting, Mum? Just tell us so we can put an end to all this horror.'

'I'll tell you where it is as soon as I get the assurance I'm after from Gregory and the premier.'

Joyce sat down and managed to create the impression that she'd sit like Patience on a monument until the matter had been resolved to her satisfaction. Margaret's loathing of Joyce was peaking. She was beginning to feel hot, as if she might burst into flames. She took deep breaths and rather than avert her gaze she examined Joyce from head to foot. She hoped to diminish her by identifying her physical flaws. She was disappointed because although Joyce's appearance was discouraging overall, taken one by one her features were unremarkable. With her rage unabated, she barely noticed when Gregory returned with Louisa Wetherly. The premier was immediately struck by the atmosphere in the room.

'There is an unmistakable something in the air,' she said. 'I always seem to arrive at the wrong time. I'm beginning to think it might be me. What has happened, because clearly *something* has happened?'

Gregory sighed dramatically.

'I may have to resign.'

'Impossible. The election is only weeks away. We're having no resignations and no controversies thank you very much. I don't care if you resign the day after the election, but *not* before it. I don't care if you've murdered someone.'

Before Louisa had time to say anything more,

Gregory took her by the arm, rather firmly, and led her into the dining room.

'The crisis begins here,' he said, pointing at the empty frame, and then he led Louisa back into the living room, where he pointed at Joyce, 'and ends there.'

'With a detour in the direction of Sophie White,' Phoebe said.

'I'm being blackmailed on two fronts.'

'Oh, blackmail,' Louisa said. 'We can deal with that discreetly. We do it all the time.'

'A visit from a bullet-headed Fed won't solve this,' Gregory said. 'The local police are bad enough.'

He flipped open his laptop and handed it to Louisa.

'As you know, I'd decided not to go ahead with the Archibald project, even though I'd signed a release with Sophie White. I knew she was angry and disappointed, but I underestimated *how* angry and *how* disappointed she was. She's threatening to hang this copy of my portrait in the Archibald unless the original resurfaces.'

'Where is the original?' Louisa asked.

'That was stolen by my mother-in-law,' Gregory said matter-of-factly. 'Don't ask. I'll get to that. Look at the new portrait.'

Louisa glanced at the screen and then at Gregory.

'It looks the same.'

'I'll summarise it for you. Everything is the same except that my genitals have been reduced to a believable, but inaccurate and much smaller, dimension, and I'm sorry, I know it's shallow, but I can't bear the thought that people might think that I have a very small penis when I *don't* have a very small penis. I'm not saying that I think I have a particularly remarkable penis. I don't think that. Anyway, you've seen it Louisa, the painting of it I mean, so you know it's perfectly ordinary, but within a range that isn't likely to excite discussion either way. So you see, I simply *have* to put the original in the Archibald, and the only person who knows where the original is, is Joyce, who stole it, and who won't tell us where it is unless we agree to teach creationism in schools. I think you're now fully briefed. Oh, and as a sort of full stop, Sophie White painted a tattoo of a swastika on my corona.'

'On your what?'

'The head of my penis.'

Louisa leaned towards the screen.

'She's very good, isn't she? It's got that sort of faded and rubbed look of a well-worn tattoo.'

'Yes, well, I've lost a bit of interest in her skills as an artist.'

Louisa closed the computer lid and handed it back to Gregory. In her term as premier, she'd weathered one or two scandals. Those who liked and admired her had been shaken, but hadn't abandoned her. Those who disliked her had simply had their opinions confirmed. The scandals hadn't involved her directly. They were the result of bad judgements made by colleagues within her own party. One MP had been forced to resign, and he'd announced his resignation with his wife beside him, assuring viewers that she loved and trusted him still, and that they and their children would get past this, and that her husband's resignation did not imply guilt. Gregory's problem wasn't as combustible, but all the polls suggested that the election was too close to call, and that the result might rest on a mere handful of votes. Louisa didn't want to see the word 'lewd' in a headline ever again.

'I see your dilemma, Gregory. The fact of the matter is that neither of these paintings can be put on display. There will be some kind of furore, whipped up by the gutter press, and we can have *no* furore of any size. It won't be helpful to us. So I don't care how you fix this, but I expect you to fix it. It's a problem created by you, and therefore it will be a problem solved by you. Do you understand that?'

Gregory answered like a chided schoolboy.

'Yes, of course.'

The next person to speak was Joyce, and what she said confused everyone.

'I don't think there'll be much of a furore really. Our culture is too mired in filth for that to happen. The swastika is the real problem here. That's the thing that will topple Gregory. I have no doubt at all that the moral bankruptcy of the electorate would ensure that the original, swastika-free portrait, despite it being an abject piece of debauchery, will be applauded in some circles. Some people will titter, and there'll be a flurry of interest, and some people will even celebrate what they'll see as Gregory's courage. He'll probably be returned with more votes than he got last time. This is the parlous state our democracy finds itself in.'

There was silence as people tried to unpick Joyce's strange logic. She seemed to be making a case for hanging the original picture. Phoebe thought she must have misheard her mother.

'Are you now supporting Gregory putting his portrait in the Archibald? Have you had a stroke?'

'I'm a realist, Phoebe. You should know that. The Lord moves in mysterious ways, his wonders to perform, and He has delivered the fate of this government into my hands.'

'How so?' Louisa asked.

'This artist, this … woman, I suppose … *will* release an image of her painting to the press even if you can prevent her from entering the Archibald, although I don't think you can. Your government's success is balanced precariously on the end of my son-in-law's penis.'

Hearing Joyce say 'penis' actually made Phoebe gasp.

'It's all about the swastika,' Joyce said and bestowed a wintry smile on the room.

'I'll go on national television,' Phoebe said, 'and attest to the inaccuracy and to the defamatory nature of

Sophie White's new portrait.' She looked reassuringly at Gregory. 'And not just about the tattoo — the size too. We should confront her head on and warn prospective clients about her tactics. We could end her career instead of her ending yours.'

'That would be a cataclysmic mistake,' Louisa said. 'I know you're an excellent PR person, Phoebe, but the idea of a politician's wife going on television to discuss the size of her husband's penis is too bizarre to contemplate. If you were the minister for the arts, Gregory, it wouldn't matter so much. No one expects much from the minister for the arts, but education ...'

'I wonder,' Margaret said, and her tone did have something of wonder in it, 'I wonder if what is really, truly bizarre here is that Joyce might be right. Those are words that I can't believe I'm saying out loud, in front of witnesses, but maybe she has her finger on the electorate's pulse. While we've been underestimating them, she's been estimating them. Her low opinion of them is strangely reassuring. Let's just take a moment to think this through.'

Sally clattered her way towards a chair. The carpet again muffled her passage until she emerged on its far side, where three more gunshot steps took her to a chair, where she sat down, indifferent to the disruptive power of her footwear.

Louisa wanted to believe that Joyce's diagnosis of societal turpitude was correct. It would certainly work in their favour. She, of course, didn't see these supposed values as turpitude, but the result of education and common sense. Perhaps people wouldn't be shocked by a naked portrait after all.

'When is the Archibald Prize?' she asked.

'The winning entry is announced two weeks before the election,' Gregory said.

Louisa's mind was trying to tamp down her misgivings, but she was meeting with little success. Even if the majority of people couldn't care less about an art prize, the press would love it, and go to town. She could see the sense, though, in avoiding a situation where she'd be fielding questions about the poor choice of decoration on a cabinet minister's member.

'Sally,' she said, 'you're the youngest person here. Think of yourself as a focus group. Would the sight of a naked member of parliament cause you to change your vote? I mean, of course, a painting of one. Only medical trauma professionals should have to deal with the real thing.'

'I'm not really a typical member of the electorate.'

'Nevertheless, you're young, you move about. You must have some sense of how people think.'

'If this is a focus group of people who think the way I do, I can honestly say it wouldn't change our votes. I'm not a swinging voter, though. If this naked person was on the other side of politics, I'd think he was a wanker, but I wouldn't be voting for him anyway. If he was on my side of politics, I'd think "well done, you", but I'd still think he was a bit of a wanker, and I'd also think he'd paid the artist to add a few centimetres. Sorry, Gregory. I'm just speaking on behalf of the focus group.'

'Phoebe? How about you?' Louisa asked.

'It wouldn't change my vote unless I found out he also supported duck shooting. I'd be appalled, though, at the poor PR advice he'd been given. I'd be even more appalled if he'd failed to get any PR advice if there'd been any close at hand.'

Louisa wisely hurried on.

'Margaret?'

'Definitely not. Politics before pudenda, I always say. Well I don't *always* say it. I don't even say it often. In fact, that's the first time I've said it, but I stand by it.'

Although this was hardly a representative group, Louisa was feeling reassured.

'Gregory? I need hardly ask where you stand on this.'

'Clearly not. I like to give the people in my electorate some credit.'

Giving the electorate credit wasn't something Louisa had ever thought of doing, but now wasn't the time to challenge Gregory on this.

'Joyce?'

She wasn't expecting a generous or positive answer, and she didn't get one.

'It wouldn't change my vote, because no one I'd vote for would display himself pornographically and expect to be applauded for it.'

Louisa faced Gregory.

'You've brought us to a desperate moment in our party's history. I hope you appreciate that. So far this whole ghastly situation is known only to me and you. I may seem calm, but I assure you I am very, very angry.'

Louisa had a tendency to describe her emotions rather than enact them, but occasionally a burst of white-hot rage would escape her. It happened unpredictably, and it happened now.

'Joyce!'

Everyone felt a physical jolt.

'As premier of this state, I insist that you produce that wretched portrait! I will not have my campaign derailed by Gregory's penis!'

After the initial shock, Joyce settled back into stoic, granitic rectitude.

'I will produce the great abomination when you produce a guarantee that my petition will be distributed among the members of parliament.'

'Fine,' Louisa said. Petitions were a dime a dozen, and easily ignored or dismissed.

'And I want Gregory to raise the issues contained in it for serious debate in the House.'

'Fine,' Louisa said again. Gregory's career was essentially over, so there was no further point in either cultivating or manipulating him.

'What? No!' Gregory was stung into an exclamation.

'All Joyce wants is for you to organise a debate.'

'But it will look like it's an issue worthy of debate, and it will look like I'm in favour of it. You're throwing me under a bus here, Louisa.'

'I'm not throwing you under a bus, Gregory. It's your bus, you hired the driver, and you're walking under it.'

Phoebe was aware, even if Gregory wasn't, that Louisa Wetherly now detested him, and that even if he won his seat he'd be demoted to the back bench, and that his fellow members would be encouraged to ostracise and isolate him. Would his nerve hold long enough to marshal support and challenge Louisa for the leadership? She knew that this was his ambition. He'd always said he hoped to do it from a position of strength and from within the cabinet. She looked at him and wanted to cry. How could such an intelligent man be so naive?

When Gregory had first gone into parliament, he'd spoken often about the difference he thought he could make if he were ever to rise to the position of premier. Phoebe went along with him and smiled and agreed that he'd make a great premier. She never told him that she didn't believe his ambition was achievable. He lacked the essential quality of ruthlessness. Louisa Wetherly had this in spades. Phoebe could hear it in her voice and see it in her posture. Gregory could only see more-worthy qualities in Louisa, like confidence and admirable assertiveness. This was a weakness in him, underpinned perhaps by decency, which made him vulnerable.

'I want the matter discussed before this election,' Joyce said. 'We're going to field a candidate in the seat of Luttrall. We won't put anyone up against Gregory in his own seat, but Luttrall is a marginal seat and we think we may have a chance there.'

She paused for effect.

'We will of course need your preferences to flow to our candidate. We will return the favour to your candidate in that seat.'

'Who,' Louisa asked very slowly, 'are "we"?'

'Oh we're not a party as such. We are committed Christians who are supporting our independent candidate. He's a family man, with seven children and a fine determination to root out the paganism of science from the school curriculum.'

'We have just entered uncharted territory of the weird and grotesque,' Margaret said. 'I know you're serious, and yet I can't grasp how delusional you must actually be.'

Louisa, who was now confident that her body had expelled its hot fury, spoke in her reclaimed professional tones.

'Joyce, you must surely understand that my party could never endorse such a conservative and untested candidate. We are a progressive party. Our preferences will not flow to a person who disavows science. It's out of the question. Even our opponents wouldn't give their first preferences to such an extremist.'

The faintest smile leaked into Joyce's face and then sank back into the obscurity where all her rare and fleeting smiles lurked. Phoebe had thought she'd seen the worst of her mother, but this new, politically engaged mother was a kraken.

'How do you square all this with your conscience, Mum?'

'My conscience is clear, Phoebe. My conscience is always clear.'

Sally's fascination with the dynamics at play had been replaced since Louisa's arrival with agitation, and Joyce had now morphed from curiosity to monster.

'You've stolen a valuable work of art,' Sally said, 'and you're blackmailing my brother. That's one elastic conscience.'

Joyce turned to Sally and bestowed upon her a look which said, 'I find your lesbianism disgusting.' That at any rate is what Sally read into the glance.

'I've stolen nothing,' Joyce said, 'and if you want to beat the devil, sometimes you have to play by his rules.'

Gregory put his head in his hands.

'Jesus Christ.'

'DO NOT BLASPHEME!' Joyce roared.

'WHERE IS MY PAINTING?' Gregory roared back.

An appalled silence followed. No one had ever heard him raise his voice to this pitch before. It was startling but not at all frightening. Phoebe was pleased that he'd directed this blast at her mother. Maybe now, after all these years, he'd stop leaping to her defence. Maybe now he'd stop indulging her as a quaint anachronism who meant no harm.

'I'm waiting for a guarantee from the premier of this state,' Joyce said, and her quiet voice was somehow more ominous and unsettling than her roar.

'Wait a minute!' Phoebe said. 'You said the painting is still in the house, or were you lying about that too?'

'I wasn't lying, Phoebe. I do not lie. I never lie.'

Phoebe's eyes widened.

'There are a limited number of places in this house where you could hide an object of that size.' She looked from Margaret to Gregory to Sally. 'We can find it. This is easy. Gregory, Sally, take upstairs. Margaret and I will search down here.'

Sally rose to her feet, clattered to the carpet, stepped into its brief, blessed silence, and clattered upstairs with Gregory. Louisa didn't join the search. She remained in the living room with Joyce.

'You're a determined sort of woman, aren't you, Joyce? It's an admirable quality in a bright person, and a dangerous one in a fool. Maybe you should have hidden the painting off-site. When they find it, you'll have nothing to bargain with.'

'They won't find the painting, Louisa. Don't mistake me for a fool. The balance of power hasn't shifted in your favour. Your civilised demeanour is wafer thin, isn't it?'

Louisa had no illusions about how much of what she presented to the world was performance and how much was her true self.

'No one's demeanour would survive exposure to you, Joyce. You're a human sandblaster. However, I didn't get to be premier of this state by batting my eyelids at my colleagues. I got here by making them realise that when they speak to me they'd better be wearing a cricket protector. I know about power, Joyce. If I enter into any sort of negotiation with you, you'd better know that it will be to serve my interests, not yours.'

'Your power is nothing. My hand is moved by the power of God. I'm not impressed by the puny thing you call political power. They won't find the painting, not without my help, and they won't get my help unless I get what I want. If you want a lesson in power, look to God, not to parliament.'

'You could be charged with theft. You do realise that.'

'I'd have to steal something first.'

Louisa had nowhere to go, so she said rather weakly, 'And you call yourself a Christian.'

Joyce narrowed her eyes slightly.

'I'm not a wet Christian, Louisa. I don't believe in a smiley God who likes guitars in church. My God is hard, unyielding, demanding — above all, demanding. A God who created maggots and parasites isn't interested in patting us on the head when we do what we think are good things. Our reward is to win a place outside this vale of tears, not find comfort and consolation within it. Vengeance is mine, sayeth the Lord. What He's never said is, "Sing me a song."'

Phoebe returned to the living room and stood with her hands on her hips.

'I've looked everywhere downstairs, including the garage. Nothing.'

Margaret joined her.

'I even looked in the freezer and the knife drawer,' she said.

Phoebe wanted to cry, but she certainly wasn't going to give her mother that satisfaction, and besides, it would have no effect on Joyce. If she'd learned one thing growing up, it was that Joyce was unmoved by the emotions of others, a fact that made Phoebe wonder if her mother had the pathology of a psychopath — without a propensity for killing, but not perhaps without the capacity for it.

'How can you do this, Mum? How can you put Gregory and me through this?'

It was a useless tilt.

'I'm engaging with the political process, Phoebe. It was Gregory who forced my hand. I am not an unreasonable person, and I think you'll find that I am willing to negotiate. You may not think so, but I do understand give and take.'

'You've certainly got a firm grip on take,' Phoebe said.

The idea that Joyce might be amenable to negotiation struck Louisa as unlikely. Negotiation required subtlety and a willingness to compromise. Joyce exhibited neither of these qualities. Nevertheless, she said, 'I'm listening, Joyce.'

Joyce's face already looked triumphant, which made Louisa regret her remark.

'Good,' Joyce said. 'I think we've reached the pointy end of discussions. I've deliberately left a bit of wriggle room, for negotiation purposes, and to demonstrate that I'm prepared to make some sacrifices. Here's what I'm prepared to do.'

She paused.

'I will withdraw the petition and the demand for a parliamentary debate.'

She waited to see if anyone appreciated the size of this compromise. She turned to Phoebe.

'I won't ask Gregory to support a parliamentary debate.'

'I'm withholding my applause, Mum.'

'And you'll do these things in exchange for what, Joyce?' Louisa asked, although she knew what was coming.

'I want your party's first-preference endorsement of our candidate in the seat of Luttrall, that's all.'

'The seat is even more marginal than Gregory's seat. I'm afraid my party will never endorse your choice of candidate. It would be electoral suicide. We'd be a laughing stock. I won't expose my colleagues to having to defend the endorsement at every press call. They're hostile enough as it is. The distraction from our policies would be catastrophic.'

Joyce had exhausted her capacity to negotiate.

'Those are my terms, and I've given up a lot to come to them. It's of no real consequence to me, in fact, whether you accept them or not. Our candidate will stand, with or without your support. We may stand one against Gregory if it comes to that. And if I may venture a prediction, Gregory's swastika'd penis will ensure that he loses his seat, and you and your cricket-protected colleagues will lose office.'

The cool ruthlessness in Joyce's voice made her pronouncement seem somehow alarmingly perspicacious. Margaret's nerves were jangled by it, and to soothe herself as much as to soothe Louisa, she said, 'No one's going to vote for a lunatic creationist, Louisa — if you'll pardon the tautology. And tucked away in an obscure electorate like Luttrall — I have no idea where it is, for example — who'll notice where your preferences go? However marginal that seat is, there's no danger that this religious nut job will get elected, and if *his* preferences flow back to you, who knows, that might secure a win there for you. *That* would be a delicious irony.'

Joyce's face was immobile with indifference.

'If Gregory and Sally haven't found the painting,'

Margaret continued, 'maybe you should think about Joyce's terms. I know that will go against every decent fibre in your body, but this is the realpolitik we find ourselves in.'

Louisa breathed in and out deeply.

'Surely they'll have found the painting,' she said, 'and this part of the nightmare can end. Maybe, *maybe* it could be managed without a brouhaha being made about it.'

'I don't intend making a brouhaha,' said Joyce. 'We will stand our candidate and leave the result up to God, not the press.'

'So your candidate won't be giving interviews?' Louisa said, mildly astonished at Joyce's naivety.

'We are well aware that he wouldn't be given a sympathetic hearing. People of faith are treated like sideshow freaks. There will be a reckoning. We will put up our man and make no noise. They also serve who only stand and wait.'

Margaret's impulse was to slap the piousness out of Joyce, but she resisted, recognising that the sight of her rolling around the floor with Joyce would be unedifying.

Gregory and Sally returned at that point, and each of them was empty-handed.

'It's not upstairs,' Gregory said, 'and I looked in the roof space, for God's sake. I looked everywhere, under sheets and under mattresses.'

'I'm impressed, Joyce,' Sally said. 'Unless you found

a way into the wall cavity, you've pulled off a decent magic trick, worthy of David Copperfield. It's got me stumped.'

'Is it in a wall cavity, Mum? Are we going to have to knock through the plaster to retrieve it? Because if that's what we have to do, you're paying for it.'

'Your hostility is unbecoming, Phoebe. It's not in the wall space. Retrieving it will cost nothing. Not retrieving it, on the other hand, will cost Gregory a great deal.'

'All right,' Louisa said. 'I hope I know when to capitulate and when to hold out. I think what you've done and what you're doing is unconscionable, but there's more at stake here than our pride. You win.'

Gregory was panicky. 'Wait. What? What does she win?'

'While you've been upstairs, Gregory, Joyce and I have been engaging in a bit of negotiation around how to proceed through the mess you've created. Joyce and her cronies are putting up a candidate in the seat of Luttrall. This person's signature is no doubt on that petition?'

'It is.'

'And therefore we may assume that his political views are indistinguishable from Joyce's.'

'I have said as much.'

'Wouldn't such a person be an ornament in the House? However, I've agreed to direct our preferences to this person in that seat and *only* in that seat. Joyce has

agreed to take her petition off the table and relieve you
of the job of promoting it. I'm hoping that in the hurly-
burly of the election no one will notice this preference
anomaly in one seat. Luttrall has a high percentage of
long-term unemployed and more caravan parks than
is good for the DNA security of any suburb. So, one
creationist probably won't register as being of much
interest. I believe there's a Shooting Party candidate and
a Save the Pitbull candidate as well. Most people in that
electorate think that wearing shoes is elitist.'

Louisa's public persona as a politician with slightly
left-of-centre views was prone to veer off course in
private.

'Is there any chance of this person being elected?'
Gregory asked. 'Because if there is, I don't want that on
my conscience.'

Joyce hunched her shoulders in eloquent dismissal
of the idea that Gregory might have a conscience.

'Luttrall is a marginal seat,' Louisa said, 'but no seat
is *that* marginal.'

Sally was feeling uncomfortable and wasn't
convinced by Louisa's confidence about this.

'I don't know. Stranger things have happened. You're
rolling dice here.'

Before Sally could convince Louisa to have second
thoughts, Joyce said, 'Good. Excellent. Everything is
settled.'

Louisa faltered for just a moment before she said,

'All right, Joyce. You have your guarantee, and you have witnesses to back it up. So, where is the painting?'

Joyce folded her arms and sat back in her chair, where she allowed herself a few seconds of silent pleasure in her victory.

'Well?' Phoebe said.

'It's here. In this room.'

'No it isn't, Mum. We looked in here. Unless you've ruined it by folding it into quarters and putting it under one of the seat cushions. It's useless to us if it's ruined. So if that's what you've done, the deal is off.'

'I haven't folded it or damaged it. It exists in all its hideous completeness.'

All eyes swept the room as if last-minute surveillance might pick up a corner of the painting poking out from somewhere. Nothing.

'Mum?' Phoebe said again.

'The painting is where it, and all filth, belongs — being trodden underfoot.'

'Underfoot?' Margaret said.

It took a moment for the penny to drop, and it was Sally who got there first.

'It's under the carpet!' she said. She leapt up, clattered to the edge and lifted a corner.

'There it is! It's been under our noses all this time.'

'It's been under your feet,' Joyce said. 'I'll thank you not to uncover that vile object until I've left. Phoebe, call me a taxi.'

Gregory moved forward and with angry defiance he rolled the carpet back to reveal the portrait. Joyce stood up and turned her back.

'It's like showing a crucifix to a vampire, isn't it?' Margaret said.

Louisa looked down at the picture, hoping to reassure herself that it wasn't as explicit as she'd remembered it being. There it was, though: Gregory's penis at the centre of the image. It was inescapably the focal point. It simply wasn't possible to look at the painting and *not* see it. She was suddenly, once more furious.

'You know what you should call this, Gregory?' she said. 'You should call it *The Education Minister's Cock*, because that's essentially what this is.'

Gregory blanched, and because her back was turned, no one saw the fleeting smile that crossed Joyce's face.

'There's no need to call a taxi, Phoebe,' Louisa said. 'I have a car waiting outside. I'll drop Joyce home. Think of it as a political rather than a social courtesy.'

Joyce unexpectedly agreed to Louisa's offer. An unholy alliance was still an alliance.

'You might care to tell me something about your candidate. You'll need to make sure he's had a recent police check.'

Joyce didn't rise to the offensive suggestion implied by Louisa's remark. Instead she bade curt farewells and headed for the front door. Before she reached it, Gregory said, 'I'll contact Sophie White and let her know that her blackmail has been effective — as effective as yours, Joyce.'

Joyce paused and faced him.

'What you call blackmail, I call an effective political strategy. I leave here with a clear conscience, knowing that I've done God's work. If I've offended anybody in the process, I can't say I'm sorry. If you find God's work offensive, you find God offensive.'

She took a step forward in Phoebe's direction.

'You know my door is always open, Phoebe. When you return to the Lord, you can return to me.'

'Neither option is attractive, Mum. I prefer an open mind to an open door.'

Joyce turned and left. Louisa was genuinely appalled by this exchange, and embarrassed by what she took to be its rawness. She was wrong about this. Whatever raw force it might have had for Phoebe had dissipated long ago, so that it now had no more power than white noise.

'Goodbye, Gregory, Margaret, Sally, Phoebe. Let's hope that Joyce's low opinion of the electorate is correct. Oh, Gregory, you'll need to organise a strategy to deal with any Archibald hysteria. I'm going to be very hands off about it, and I warn you, I won't be celebrating your decision. When I'm asked, and I *will* be asked, I'm going to say I advised against it, and I'm frankly going to say that I think the painting is truly awful. Phoebe is in PR. I'm sure you'll sort something out. My minimum expectation is that you inflict *minimum* damage on the government, and I'd appreciate it if you'd turn up at any events between now and the election fully clothed.'

She followed Joyce out the front door and found her already ensconced in the back seat of the car. She'd have to speak to Archie about this. It amounted to a security breach, after all.

In the living room, Sally said that she'd contact Carol and let her know that the mystery had been solved.

'Ask her to pass that on to Jack Craig. I don't want to speak to him. I'm so angry with Joyce that I've got half a mind to lay charges of vandalism against her. She did cut the picture out of the frame.'

Phoebe put her arm around him.

'You've finally reached the point of disliking my mother. I call that personal growth.'

'That was a terrible thing your mother said to you,' Margaret said. 'My God, she's a hard woman.'

'Faith creates monsters. I don't take it personally anymore, I really don't. We each live in hope that the other will see the light.'

'I think you have very different ideas about light. Joyce's light will fry you. You know, I feel quite wrung out. You must be exhausted, Phoebe. I remember when I was pregnant with Sally I was tired all the time.'

'What about when you were pregnant with Gregory?' Sally said. 'I suppose that was just unmitigated joy.'

'I don't know what it was, darling, but you were an

exhausting fetus. You were quite an exhausting child too as it happens.'

There was no point in pursuing this conversation, for Sally at least. She recognised that her mother had slipped into a familiar mood where she said things for effect, as if she were testing them for a stand-up act. Rational discussion wasn't possible. Margaret would simply accuse Sally of lacking a sense of humour. Sally had sufficient self-confidence to know that all she lacked was her mother's sense of humour.

'I'm heading off,' Margaret said, 'but we'll need to reconvene to sort out how we're going to deal with the inevitable fallout from the Archibald. It's going to be on the front page of the tabloids with a stupid emoji over the genitals. That *is* going to happen, and I'm not sure what's worse, a modesty emoji or no emoji.'

'It might not even make the final cut, Mum,' Gregory said. 'We're all assuming it will just be waved through to the hang. It might be rejected.'

In a rather repressive tone, Sally said, 'Sophie White always makes the final cut, and the Archibald committee isn't going to pass up the publicity this will guarantee.'

Gregory nodded his agreement.

'The most galling thing about this,' he said, 'is that I'll have to defend her, and I feel so betrayed by her.'

'We can survive this,' Margaret said, 'although I have trepidations.'

'There's no need to worry about me, Mum. I went

into this with my eyes open.' He caught Phoebe's eye. 'Or at least I thought they were open. They've now been prised wide open.'

'It's not you I'm worried about,' Margaret said. 'It's Joyce. She terrifies me. I think she's a dangerous woman, and that's not hyperbole.'

'I think you can relax, Mum,' Sally said. 'Even in the unlikely event that Joyce's candidate got elected, he'd be found in bed with the wrong person in no time at all. Fundamentalists always have sexual peccadilloes they can't help indulging, and regretting. It's all about self-loathing dressed up as evangelising.'

'Thank you, Sally. That's very reassuring, although frankly simplistic, although in a way I'm sure you're essentially right. It all comes back to sex, doesn't it?'

Margaret gathered herself for departure. She kissed Sally on the cheek and embraced Phoebe.

'Fortunately, the unborn child won't remember anything that was said here today, although God knows in the future they might find a way of recovering fetal memories. Wouldn't that be a nightmare?'

She placed her hands on Gregory's shoulders.

'Gregory, darling, you know you can rely on me to say the right thing should the journalists come calling, but we do need to sit down, all of us, and get some coaching from Phoebe about the approach we should take.'

'Yes, of course, Mum. No one can afford to go rogue

on this. It's all my fault, I know that. I hope I'm big enough to admit that.'

While Gregory walked Margaret to her car, Sally said, 'Is anything wrong, Phoebe? Your voice went a bit funny just now when you were saying goodbye.'

Phoebe bent down and rolled back a section of the carpet so that Gregory's face was exposed.

'Look at the expression on his face, Sally. What do you see?'

'He looks smug. Confident, but smug. It's a bit hard to tell looking down on it like this. What did you say earlier?'

'I said that Sophie White had made him look venal. Now I also think he looks ambitious and ruthless.'

'Really?'

Sally looked hard at the picture.

'I don't see that. Pompous maybe.'

'When I saw this for the very first time, I was furious with Sophie White because I thought she didn't like Gregory and so she gave him an unflattering look. Now I think she might be a very good artist and that she painted what she actually saw.'

She re-covered the painting with the carpet.

'Were you ever frightened of Gregory when you were growing up, Sally?'

The question startled Sally.

'Frightened of him? No. No, of course not. Frightened? How do you mean? If you mean did he ever physically threaten me, absolutely not … Has Gregory been threatening you, Phoebe? Or worse?'

'What? Oh Lord no. He can be annoying, but he rarely even raises his voice, and then it's directed at uncooperative, inanimate objects.'

'Than why did you ask such a question?'

Before Phoebe could answer, Gregory returned, and stood in the centre of the room and exhaled noisily. He realised he was standing on his portrait, but instead of moving he remained where he was.

'This is going to be a more interesting election than most of them,' Sally said. 'Your profile is going to go through the roof. Are you prepared for that? You'll have to be very brave.'

The sight of Gregory standing, legs apart, arms folded, like some colossus astride the world seemed to ignite something in Phoebe.

'It's not Gregory who'll have to be brave, Sally. It's the rest of us. He'll be fine. He's an exhibitionist. He's not the victim here.'

'I'm not an exhibitionist,' Gregory said. 'That just isn't true. I am, however, in favour of artistic expression. I can see now, though, that Sophie White exploited that for her own purposes, and I have to pay the price for her ambition to win the Archibald Prize.'

'She's just the artist. Of course she's ambitious about her picture. But you seem to be confusing her ambitions with your own.'

Sally was now feeling hideously uncomfortable. She could see that Phoebe and Gregory were on the edge of what might be a nasty fight. She hated it when couples fought in front of her. It was inevitable that either Phoebe or Gregory would call on her to support her or his position.

'This might be a good time to leave,' she said. 'I feel you two have stuff to discuss which doesn't need an audience.'

Before either of them could protest, Sally kissed each of them on the cheek, a gesture that signalled unequivocally that she was leaving.

'Stay strong,' she said.

'Oh. All right. I hope we weren't embarrassing you,' Phoebe said.

'Not at all,' Sally lied.

'You don't need to worry about Gregory and me. We're solid. This isn't a George and Martha situation. I may be mightily pissed off, but we're solid, especially now that we're going to be three.'

'Yes, we should be fussing over you.'

'I'm not bothered about that. Both the baby and I are perfectly comfortable with not being fussed over. Gregory is the needy one here, not me. And he's created a situation where all his needs are met.'

Sally felt thwarted in her escape attempt.

'No. I'm not going to argue with you, Phoebe,' Gregory said. 'I'm too exhausted, and also I don't know

what you could possibly mean. How could losing Louisa
Wetherly's support meet any need of mine?'

'That rather depends on whose support you're
courting. I know all about dirty politics, Gregory. Tell
me honestly, have you orchestrated this whole thing so
that Louisa dumps you and frees you from the taint of
being one of her supporters? Is it easier to challenge her
for her job after being dumped rather than after simply
resigning?'

Gregory was silent, and his face didn't reveal whether
he was horrified by Phoebe's suggestion, or shocked by
her insight.

'That would be dirty and convoluted politics,' he
said. 'I always thought that you believed in my integrity.'

'Oh I do believe in your integrity, but I also think
you've learned to use it like a sort of carbon offset. An
integrity offset. You sequester it, save it up for a rainy day.'

'My level of discomfort is now at an all-time high,'
Sally said. She realised that she'd entered the awful
sphere of having become invisible to an arguing couple.
It was only a matter of time before one of them 'saw'
her and demanded that she declare her allegiance, or
otherwise.

'Why are you attacking me, Phoebe?' Gregory
said, and it was obvious that this was an attempt to
distract her from her line of argument. 'I'm feeling
very vulnerable at the moment, and I feel like you're
attacking me.'

Phoebe turned to Sally.

'See what I mean? Needy. Don't you agree, Sally?'

Fortunately, at this stage it was a rhetorical question.

'I'm not attacking you, Gregory. I'm angry with you, and I'm pretty sure I'm right about your strategy, and I disagree with it, and I'm mightily disappointed that you didn't run any of this by me. That makes me feel like you don't respect my skills. So, angry, yes. Attacking, no, and before you say anything, I'll tell you what *really* makes me angry.'

'Please, enlighten me.'

'I know a great deal about public relations. It's what I do.'

Gregory held up a hand as if to stop Phoebe from further explanation.

'Look, if this is about your firm's tender for that job last year, you know the conflict of interest would have created a shitstorm.'

Phoebe put her hands on her hips.

'It's not about that. Of course it's not about that. I advised the partners to not bother putting in that tender, as you very well know. They ignored my advice. I ran it by you at the time, and I agreed with you one hundred per cent. However, not once in the last six months, not once, have *you* asked for advice on anything. Why?'

Gregory's voice was in danger of becoming shrill.

'If you're talking about the bloody portrait, I wanted it to be, I thought it would be, a surprise. If I'd consulted with you first, it wouldn't have been much of a surprise, would it?'

'If you'd consulted with me, it would never have been painted.'

Sally felt compelled to speak.

'I'm still here and I'm still uncomfortable.'

Phoebe and Gregory ignored her.

Phoebe said, 'It had nothing to do with it being a surprise. You knew that if you told me what you were planning to do, I'd know what your real motive was, and that it had nothing to do with art.'

Gregory's mouth opened slightly, guppy-like.

'Oh my Lord. You're jealous. You really are. You think there was something between Sophie White and me.'

'OH, STUPID, STUPID MAN.'

Sally flinched and a small 'Oh no' escaped her. Gregory took a step backward as if the words had sufficient physical force to propel him.

Phoebe took a few deep breaths and continued.

'I'm sorry. I'm calm now. All calm. I won't dignify what you just said with a response, but I will say this. You thought you were in control of all this. You thought you were smarter than Sophie White. Well you're not. All along, you wanted that thing in the Archibald because you thought and you still think that people will like it and applaud you.'

Gregory looked like he was about to interrupt.

'Let me finish, Gregory. It's more complicated than just that. You also knew that Louisa Wetherly would be angry enough about it to want to distance herself from you. You haven't trusted me enough to tell me why you want that to happen. Now *that* makes me angry, because it's about your future, and it was my understanding that our futures were interlinked.'

There was such focus in Phoebe's emotion that Gregory was beginning to feel nervous, and his nervousness was evident in his voice.

'You're making a simple decision to have my portrait painted into an elaborate Machiavellian plot.'

'Oh, Gregory, it's so much more banal than that.'

She paused deliberately for effect.

'It's just about ambition. That's all it is. Ambition. What you didn't count on was Sophie White seeing right through you and putting all of that into your face.'

'No, Phoebe. What I didn't count on was your mother, whose actions came close to destroying my career.'

'Which is odd, because the one person you can always count on is Mum.'

Sally then did a very peculiar thing. She clapped her hands twice, so that it sounded less like a request for silence and order and more like weirdly truncated applause.

'I have now reached spontaneous-combustion levels of embarrassment, and lycra has a low melting point, so I'm going.'

Gregory moved to her and kissed his sister on the cheek.

'I'm sorry we embarrassed you, Sally. It's nothing really. It's just a silly tiff. That's right, isn't it, Phoebe? A tiff.'

'Oh, yes,' Phoebe said stonily. 'That's all it is. Just a silly, meaningless tiff.'

# THREE WEEKS LATER

The first eyes to fall upon portraits entered into the Archibald Prize belong to the packers — the gallery staff who unpack the paintings and prepare them for their rapid passage past the ten trustees of the Art Gallery of New South Wales. The winner is decided by these trustees. There is also a people's choice winner, and a winner chosen by the packers. The Packing Room Prize is never controversial. The packers like portraits that look like the subject, and they are susceptible to the female nude. The male nude rarely holds their gaze. It is true that in 2015 Marcus Wills' *El cabeceo* made them pause, but it might have been the Rubenesque rear view of the wife rather than the startlingly realistic front view of the husband that caught their eyes. They seem unfussed by the fact that a packing-room winner has never gone on to win the big prize.

When the head packer ran his eyes over Gregory Buchanan, his first words were, 'Fucking hell.' His more considered response was, 'Sophie White is a bloody good painter. She's smart. Whoever this clown is who posed for her, though, he's dumb as a box of hammers.' He checked his notes on the painting. 'He's a pollie! This should be retitled *Career Suicide*.' He shook his head, whistled, and said, 'Next!'

Had Sophie White been privy to this process, she would have been relieved to have been passed over for the Packing Room Prize. Not that she despised the prize; she didn't. She'd often preferred the Packing Room Prize to the Archibald winner, and she particularly liked it when the Packing Room Prize went to a portrait that had failed to make it past the trustees into the final selections. However, her goal was the Archibald, so the lesser prize simply wouldn't do.

The process of winnowing Archibald entries down from many hundreds to the final fifty or so is known to be brutal and swift. The firing squad of ten trustees, the majority of whom are not directly involved in the business of art — it would be unkind to characterise them as knowing what they like — take their seats in a row, and one by one the entries are paraded before them. Whether or not a painting is good or bad may well be an objective judgement, but a dud is a dud, and a suburban painter's portrait on velvet of Kylie Minogue is unlikely to proceed. It's even more unlikely that Ms Minogue sat for the portrait, which is a requirement for entry. Having attended a concert is not considered a legitimate sitting.

Sophie White had made it through to the final

fifty twice in her short career. She was a name. She was certainly known to the two artists who usually sat on the board. She knew how this worked. She knew that she wouldn't nab the top prize until she'd been through the apprenticeship of losing. In her first two forays, she'd hoped only to win the People's Choice award. That purse was just a few thousand dollars — well short of the $100,000 first prize.

She'd been strategic in her choice of subjects, knowing that the people who came to the gallery and cast their vote were more interested in the subject than in the painting. She'd visited the Art Gallery of New South Wales many times during the runs of the exhibitions in which her work was hanging, and she'd followed them to some of their regional installations. She liked to listen as people expressed their ill-informed opinions of the pictures they were looking at. This confirmed all of her suspicions (she would have called them certainties) about the general public. She always took a notebook with her where she recorded the most egregious of these remarks. She liked to flick through them from time to time just to top up the vitriol in her tank.

'I think the sofa is OK. At least you can tell it's a sofa. Who's the person sitting on it? Is it a person? It's so shit I'm surprised it didn't win.'

'I hate that dress! And those shoes! What was she thinking?'

'He needs a haircut. Or is that a hat? Did this person pass painting school? Maybe he was expelled.'

Sophie ought to have been pleased that her portraits excited mostly admiration, but she genuinely loathed the people who said, 'Gorgeous.' 'Sarah Snook is so beautiful.' 'It looks just like a photograph.' 'Oh, I love that necklace.' 'I saw her in a café once.'

These were the same people whose votes propelled her to win the People's Choice award. To be admired by this dreadful mob was both thrilling and appalling. She knew of course that the win really belonged to Sarah Snook. Very few people went away thinking that Sophie White was a great artist. They went away thinking that Sarah Snook was a great beauty.

The sloughing process of the initial cull was coolly efficient, like brushing dandruff from a shoulder. A few seconds were lavished on each painting, and eight hundred became two hundred in the course of a wearisome day. Sophie White's enormous portrait of Gregory Buchanan was held in place in the first round for far longer than any other picture. The trustees exchanged looks, and eyebrows were raised. It went through to the next round, unchallenged. Discussions were reserved for the second round.

It was in the second round that Sophie White's painting hit its first snag. Four of the trustees were frankly repelled by it, and one, a man who'd made millions in a tech startup, wanted to know how anyone could live with this thing hanging on the wall. This initiated a sharp rebuke from one of the artists on the board, who found it worrying that her fellow board member seemed unclear about the distinction between art and decoration. Unused to being rebuked on any matter, the tech entrepreneur countered that art should uplift, that it should bring joy. This caused a flurry of discussion and outrage up and down the line of trustees.

'The Marie Kondo approach to art,' someone said. 'That's not a world I want to live in. I don't want to get my art at IKEA. I want to be disturbed, challenged, shocked, appalled by a picture.'

'Christ. I can get all that at home on most nights.'

'Maybe there's gallery art and living-room art. I'd stand in front of a Bacon or a Freud in a gallery, but they're not the first thing I want to see before breakfast.'

The trustees had been sufficiently schooled not to waste time by arguing whether or not a portrait needed to be a likeness. Most of them thought this was pretty much the bare-minimum requirement, but saying this out loud was a recipe for accusations of cultural imperialism and art-historical ignorance. Everyone knew Picasso's riposte to the accusation that his portrait of Gertrude Stein looked nothing like her. 'It will,' he said, and time proved him right. That Sophie White's portrait of Gregory Buchanan looked like Gregory Buchanan — several board members googled him to check — wasn't in dispute. If he'd been wearing a suit, Sophie White's name, and the technical skill shown, might have taken it into the final fifty. As it was, its bracing nakedness rather took the breath away. Its nod to Bronzino was appreciated by the famously tetchy art critic on the board, who pointed out that the focus-pulling positioning of the penis was a stroke of genius that elevated the picture above the level of an illustration for a glossy magazine article — which is what, in his view, most photorealist portraits looked like. This picture wasn't just about technique, he said. It was daring. Resistance remained, with one member reminding the board that their lack of expertise was precisely what made them ideal judges. Theirs was an opinion unimpeded by knowledge. It was raw and honest.

'So you're saying that ignorance is a synonym for honesty?'

Realising the Trumpian nature of his remark, the member who'd made it immediately backed down and said that he'd 'misspoken', and that of course he wasn't making this claim. His tangled clarification was unconvincing, and more than one member privately determined to take no further account of this man's opinion.

The need to continue the cull in the second round meant that Sophie White's portrait was moved into the next round, where further discussion would take place.

There were more pauses in this second round where

the artists on the board argued for a few contemporary pieces that looked like the bastard offsprings of Basquiat and Cy Twombly. One of these got through, despite one trustee declaring that its title, *John Smiling*, could hardly be verified given that it seemed to be a painting of the back of John's head. This was seen by some as a masterstroke because it required 'us, the viewers, to imagine John's face and impose a smile upon it'.

'But it could have been called *John Weeping*, or *John Screaming*, or *John Doing God Knows What*,' an exasperated trustee said.

'Yes,' said one of the artists, 'but it wasn't.'

That was felt to put the tin hat on that line of discussion, and the next painting was carried in.

When the hunt for fifty had been whittled down to one hundred, Gregory Buchanan was once again propped up against the wall for a close perusal. This time, the trustees left their seats and examined it closely.

'This Gregory Buchanan bloke, anyone heard of him?'

Nobody had. He wasn't a politician from New South Wales. They were surprised to learn that he was a sitting member in another state, up for imminent re-election.

'He's the minister for education,' someone said, doing a quick google again.

'You have to be kidding me.'

One of the female trustees, a woman who'd been decorated with an Order of Australia and two honorary doctorates, and who'd proved over several Archibald selections that she was unshockable and willing to take advice from the art experts, said, 'Part of this man's duty is to stand before audiences of primary-school and secondary-school children, including, I imagine, children in religious schools.'

'Oh, that is so brilliant,' someone said. 'That hadn't occurred to me.'

'I wasn't celebrating that fact,' the woman said. 'What I can't understand is why he would agree to this. He's not just pushing the envelope, is he — he's setting it on fire.'

'What are we looking at here? Courage? Look at his face.'

'You have to remember to do that, don't you?'

'I see a lot of things in that face — which is a testament to Sophie White's skill — but the one thing I don't see is courage.'

It was unanimously agreed that courage wasn't a flattering unction that could be laid to Gregory Buchanan's soul. The painting so divided the trustees that they had no choice but to let it through to the final fifty. For some of them, the motivation for its inclusion wasn't so much a question of art. It was more in the hope that its presence might result in a change of career for the sitter.

The hang for the Archibald finalists inevitably leads to speculation before the winner is announced.

Is that the winner? No, it can't be. It's hanging in the wrong place for cameras and for speeches. Is that the winner? No, not unless the trustees suffered sympathetic and simultaneous strokes. What about that one, *John Smiling*? Yes, that *has* to be a contender. It's well placed for the photo call.

Gregory Buchanan's portrait was too big to tuck away in a corner, but pundits suggested it was simply hanging in the wrong place to win. 'Besides, look at it.' 'There's no fucking way the trustees of the Art Gallery of New South Wales are going to hand over $100,000 to the person who painted that.' 'It's a good painting,' the pundits acknowledged, 'but would the trustees want to court the controversy such a win would provoke?' They were always up for controversy, of course, but the controversies were about polite things like style, or relevance, or predictability. They tended not to be about cabinet ministers' genitalia.

Gregory genuinely thought that he was prepared for, and indifferent to, the public reaction to Sophie White's portrait. Phoebe had tried to warn him that there really was such a thing as bad publicity, and that bad publicity had a way of preying on the mind even if you tried to ignore it by switching off all media. As a politician Gregory could impose a personal media blackout for a limited time only, especially during an election campaign. The painting was everywhere, and Sophie White was everywhere. Gregory caught one of her television appearances, and he forced himself to watch as she stared down the camera and thanked him for his courage.

'Oh yes,' she said oleaginously, 'it was Gregory Buchanan's idea to be painted nude. I was unsure, but he said he wanted this to be a true collaboration, and I thank him for that. I think the result is very strong, don't you?'

'Unforgettable, certainly,' the interviewer said in a tone that suggested this wasn't necessarily a good thing and that some things are best forgotten. Sophie was on her very best behaviour, and many viewers found her charming. Many more came away with the impression that Gregory Buchanan had forced himself upon her, demanding that she stare at his naked body for hours at a time. Sophie White was diminutive; Gregory Buchanan was hulking by comparison. This looked like some form of coercive abuse.

Newspaper headlines were predictable clichés, unfunny and obvious. An eggplant, a crown, and various forms of the face emoji were the censoring panels of choice. The image wasn't censored online. It was ludicrously pixelated on some of the television coverage.

Phoebe tracked as much of the media response as

she could. There weren't enough hours in the day to see it all, and she only glanced at Reddit threads and Facebook posts. She spent more time following Twitter discussions, although most of them were dispiriting. The overwhelming feeling was that Gregory Buchanan was a knob, pure and simple. She felt like a traitor when some comments made her laugh. She didn't share these with Gregory. He'd temporarily lost his sense of humour. This was a natural consequence, Phoebe thought, of his having temporarily lost his sense of perspective.

The general consensus was that the artist who'd painted *John Smiling* could depend on picking up the $100,000. The Buchanan portrait had shock value, but didn't stand a chance. This, for both Phoebe and Gregory, was a relief. A considerable amount of damage had been done, but the klieg spotlight would move away. Gregory was looking forward to vicariously enjoying Sophie White's fury and bitterness when she lost to a painting of the back of someone's head.

Sophie White's portrait of Gregory Buchanan caused something of a furore when she was declared the winner. Her victory ensured that Gregory Buchanan, although a state politician, became the most high-profile member of any of Australia's parliaments. Cartoonists had a field day; art critics were unanimous in their derision. Sophie White and Gregory Buchanan were photographed one on either side of the portrait. They were both smiling, but the rictus quality of Gregory's smile was apparent to everyone. It was noted that the artist and her subject exchanged barely a word during the proceedings, and it was also noted that Phoebe Buchanan wasn't present at the ceremony.

In a private meeting with members of her staff, Louisa Wetherly declared that her whole election campaign was being derailed by Gregory Buchanan's cock. This appeared on Twitter within five minutes of it having been uttered, and assumed the status of a meme within hours. A state election, or 'state erection' as it was now widely described, had become more interesting to the rest of the country than it might otherwise have been.

Gregory's profile as a candidate had been raised, but it was generally agreed that even if he won his seat, the government would fail to be re-elected. He campaigned within his electorate, but refused television interviews. He'd given one, against Phoebe's advice, and it hadn't gone well. A photograph of the portrait sat superimposed behind Gregory for the duration of the interview, and it detracted mightily from the serious explication of his policies.

It had been a difficult three weeks leading to this moment when Phoebe sat down to watch the election coverage. She already knew what had happened.

Gregory had telephoned her the moment the outcome had become clear. She ought to have been there with him, and his loyal team, at the electoral office, but her morning sickness had kicked in, and she'd become convinced that it was partly due to stress, and stress was bad for the fetus.

She recognised the reporter who sat smugly in the tally room, and who was about to cross live to Gregory's electoral office. There was an incipient smile behind his attempt at gravitas.

'I think we should cross at this point to Gregory Buchanan's campaign office. I understand Mr Buchanan has conceded defeat in his seat. Mr Buchanan, can you hear me?'

There was a moment's delay, and Gregory appeared on the screen. He looked tired, but Phoebe thought he also looked composed and rather attractive.

'You must be feeling disappointed at this point, Mr Buchanan.'

'Of course. No one likes to lose an election, but that's how the democratic process works. That's how we know it's healthy. Sometimes you win and sometimes you lose. That's reassuring, isn't it? I've lost this election, but there'll be other elections, and I'm sure I can win back the confidence of my electorate. It won't take them long to discover how hollow the promises of my opponent are. I would of course like to take this opportunity to congratulate her on her win.'

'Were you surprised at the size of the swing against you?'

'We don't yet have the final figures, so I'm not prepared to speculate on that, but we'll certainly be looking at the figures very closely.'

'Were you surprised at the strong negative reaction to your portrait winning the Archibald Prize?'

Phoebe and Gregory had discussed how best to respond to this inevitable question. She hoped he would stick to the script they'd agreed on, based on several improvised interviews they'd performed.

'To be perfectly frank,' Gregory said, 'I *was* surprised by it. I thought as a community that we were a little more grown-up. I suppose I shouldn't have been surprised by the sniggering, smirking response in the media. I think we all know that the intellectual age of the tabloid press is equivalent to a not very bright, grubby, malodorous schoolboy. I was delighted for Sophie White of course.'

Phoebe put her head in her hands.

'But you must have realised that a naked portrait of a member of parliament was going to be controversial.'

'Controversial maybe, but in the end I'd hoped that people would understand it as a work of art.'

The reporter ostentatiously produced reading glasses and put them on. He took a piece of paper from the desk in front of him and brought it close.

'One critic called it, "An exercise in untrammelled narcissism, with Buchanan's naked ambition brilliantly skewered by Sophie White's unforgiving gaze. Her rendering of him is slyly subversive." How do you respond to that?'

'This isn't the time to argue the derisory state of current art criticism. The portrait will outlast the words written about it.'

'With the loss of your seat, it looks increasingly likely we'll have a hung parliament, and with a preliminary count due any minute now, it could be that the balance of power will be held by a new independent in the seat of Luttrall. He flew under the radar during the run-up to the election. Can you tell us now why your party directed its preferences to a self-confessed creationist? It's those preferences that could win him the seat. Strange bedfellows, surely?'

'I don't make decisions about preferences. That question is better directed to Louisa Wetherly.'

'So you have no idea why that deal was made. Is that right?'

'I think I've already answered that question.'

Gregory smiled unconvincingly and detached his microphone. He continued smiling, hoping to create the impression that he wasn't ending the interview in a huff.

In the tally room, the reporter looked bemused, and said, 'Mr Gregory Buchanan there. I must have said something to annoy him.' He paused, and added, 'Still, it's good to see him with his clothes on.'

Phoebe turned off the television, and wondered out

loud how much worse this could possibly get.

Her mobile rang, and the caller ID said, 'Mum'.

# ACKNOWLEDGEMENTS

It is a wonderful thing to have friends who are prepared to put aside far more pressing and important matters in order to read drafts of a manuscript. Thanks as always to Helen Murnane, Jock Serong, Jo Canham, Bill Farr, and Ted Gott. Thanks too to Henry Rosenbloom at Scribe, who has supported my writing for longer than I could have hoped. Thank you to David Golding, who edited this book and who sharpened its edges and polished the bits that were tarnished.